Lieutenant Frank Bailey, leaned back in the brown government-issue office chair and propped his feet on his desk. He felt in his shirt pocket for a cigarette. Life hadn't been the same at the Special Investigations Unit since the building went 'smoking free'. With all the fresh air to breathe his detectives and staff had more energy to gain weight, get irritable, and make his life miserable.

He peered over the top of his cluttered desk at the cop sitting across the room. Bailey knew this wasn't the typical candy ass undercover cop who runs out and gets a tattoo and an earring the first day on the job. This guy was the real thing.

The man looked as if he weighed in at about two-hundred and sixty pounds. His long beard had breakfast, lunch, and possibly happy hour debris in it, mixed liberally with chewing tobacco and spittle. His hands and arms looked as though he just changed the oil on a semi truck. His issue weapon was stuffed in his hip pocket. He didn't waste belt space for a radio or handcuffs, not that there wasn't ample space available. He just didn't need them.

NARC
in the
DARK

OTHER BOOKS BY DANIEL BYRAM

Mason's Cavalry - Vol. 1 - Border of Vengeance
Troopers and outlaws on the Arizona border circa 1910

***
Coming Soon!

**Mason's Cavalry Volume II
Guns Across the Border**
Villa's raid on Columbus, New Mexico

Tall Tales of Queen Creek
Two modern-day cowboys search for a third partner for rodeo events

Pepper Spray Primer
Personal defense guide

Blue Bird Gone
Former marine turned rescue specialist is set up by crooked politician

**Legendary Lawmen of Modern Arizona
Volume I**
Today's fighting lawmen of Arizona uphold the tradions of John Slaughter, Wyatt Earp and the Arizona Rangers. Non-fiction

NARC IN THE DARK

by

Daniel Byram

Narc in the Dark - Copyright ©1998 by Daniel Byram.
All rights reserved. No part of this book may be used, copied, reproduced or transmitted in any form or by any means, electronic or mechanical, including but not limited to photocopying, recording, or use of any information storage and retrieval system without written permission of the publisher, except for brief quotations used in critical articles or reviews. Requests for such permission should be addressed to:

Sierra West Books
PO Box 8310 - Mesa, Arizona
85214

Cover Design by:	Erika Design
Printing by:	Print Partner
Photography by:	Phil Quintana

Manufactured in the United States of America
First Edition

Daniel Byram, 1952-
    Narc in the Dark / By Daniel Byram—First Edition

ISBN 1-892798-01-8

Notice
The characters in this novel are fictitious. The characters, dialogue, and events in this book are creations of the imagination of the author. Any resemblance between the characters and events in this book and any actual event or person(s), living or dead, is purely coincidental

**Dedicated to the original
'Hogs of War'
7-24-BTW**

When soldiers deal with one another, all goes well; but when the politicians step in, the result is unadulterated stupidity.
(paraphrased)
Alexander II of Russia 1863

and

Blade's Angels

Insubordination may only be the evidence of a strong mind.
Napoleon 1817

**The author
Lieutenant Dan Byram (retired)**

CHAPTER 1

June 8th
Monday Afternoon

    Bailey's pager went off, the annoying buzz startling him out of a traffic trance as he crossed town. The fresh batteries in his pager made the vibrating message notification feel more like a chain saw strapped to his waist than a muffled hum.

    The traffic congestion on Southern Avenue during the afternoon rush hour seemed too claustrophobic to risk taking his eyes off the road to read the numbers on the tiny digital display, let alone trying to make a call while driving. He punched the pager button, and pulled off the street into the Home Depot parking lot. He squeezed the car under a small patch of shade provided by a pathetic little Palo Verde tree planted in a median strip, the only available protection from the searing Arizona sun.

    He hated stopping the car. On a good day the air conditioner blew musty smelling puffs of foul air feeling closer to warm than cold, but when the car stopped, the air blew closer to hot than warm. Any air movement seemed better than nothing in the scorching Arizona heat this time of year. It is always better to keep moving.

Bailey gave a silent prayer of thanks for not being a Patrol Division Lieutenant anymore. The thought of being stuck for another summer wearing a dark blue uniform and a kevlar bullet proof vest in 114 degree heat was appalling. Being a cop in the Valley of the Sun might be a great gig eight months a year, but the summers were almost unbearable, more akin to Hell than Bailey cared to admit. Whoever started that *but it's a dry heat* bullshit needed his ass kicked. Frowning, he turned his attention back to the numeric display on the pager.

"Dispatch?" Not good. A call from the communications center was rare since he became the head of the Special Investigations Unit (SIU) two years ago, and usually meant bad news.

He punched in the phone number for central dispatch on his cell phone and waited. A female voice came on the line, "Communications, this is Cathy speaking."

Bailey tore a piece of paper from an old Arby's fast food bag he picked up off the floorboard, then pulled a pen out of his pocket as he answered. "Hi, this is Lieutenant Bailey from SIU, I just received a page from down there."

As the words 'down there' came out of his mouth, Bailey realized he just dated himself. Dispatch is on the fourth floor of a new secured communications building now, not like the old days when it was in the basement of Headquarters. Only the old guys always say 'down there'.

I guess I'm an old guy, he thought.

After a short pause, Bill Drager, the communications shift supervisor, came on the line. "Lieutenant Bailey, Sergeant Deeson wants you to meet him at the Café Ricardo by the Hilton. He's got a jumper call. He thought you might be interested."

Bailey squirmed as he felt his stomach acid level increase. Another screwed up deal dumped on me because of a miscommunication, he thought.

"A jumper?" Are you certain he meant me? I'm dope, not the splat master. That would be Lieutenant Beltron in homicide, they always get us confused."

"Sorry boss, they specifically asked for Lieutenant Bailey, Special Investigations."

"Tell them..." Bailey paused, waiting for a diplomatic answer to come to mind, then simply responded, "...I'm enroute."

Frank punched the 'end call' button on the cell phone, put the car in gear and turned toward the parking lot exit muttering at the phone as he drove.

"Shit, maybe an overdose, but why call me for a jumper? Deeson is a moron anyway. Shit."

He flipped the cell phone shut and pulled back on the street with the air conditioner blasting.

Bailey fought the afternoon traffic and wheeled down the street on the east side of the hotel. He pulled his car up to the red curb area close to the crime scene and double parked. Out of habit, he adjusted the .45 automatic in his belt slide holster as he exited the vehicle, tugging the hem of his sport coat over the gun grip. He pulled his police ID out of his hip pocket, stepped over the yellow perimeter tape, and badged his way through the crowd. He could see paramedics working on what looked to be a badly injured man sprawled awkwardly on the ground.

My God, the man's face is mutilated, Frank thought, feeling a slight sense of revulsion. Bailey leaned over one of the medics for a closer look. The man wasn't mutilated, he had what appeared to be potato salad and a tuna sandwich smashed all over his face.

"Is this the jumper?" Bailey addressed the nearest officer.

"No sir, this is the victim."

Bailey didn't have to look at the officer's baby face to know he was a rookie. The kid sounded sincerely concerned about the injured man. Veterans don't give a shit anymore, at least not after the medics arrive.

"I'm sorry?" Confused, Bailey glared at the young officer and asked again, "Isn't the diver on a jumper call known as the victim anymore?"

"Yes sir," the youthful officer nervously replied, "But this guy didn't take the leap of faith, he is the jumpee, not the jumper."

Sergeant Deeson interrupted, strutting up to Bailey with an undeserved degree of arrogance, "Lieutenant, I'm glad you could come. This is an interesting one."

Bailey felt his blood pressure rise, he couldn't tolerate fools, especially fools who treated crime scenes like dinner parties. "What's the story Deeson, is this a jumper call or what, and why the hell am I here?"

"Well... I think it's an aggravated assault." Deeson gestured toward the injured man, "This guy laid out over there on the ground is the victim and this guy," he pointed to a disheveled old man who appeared to be about eighty years old standing beside a nearby patrol car, "Is my suspect."

"Excuse me, Sergeant, but where does the term 'jumper' come into play in this and I'm asking you for last time, WHY THE HELL AM I HERE?" Veins in Bailey's forehead and neck pulsed as he got in Deeson's face.

Deeson took a step back. The expression in his eyes indicated mental vapor lock. Apparently he just now realized he was royally pissing off the Lieutenant.

Bailey knew he was wound a little tight, but he didn't mean to take it out on Deeson, who clearly didn't realize how short a fuse Bailey was running. Deeson wasn't the sharpest pencil in the box anyway.

Bailey took a deep breath and composed himself. He extended a hand in apology, "I'm sorry Deeson, there was no call for that outburst. Would you please start from the beginning."

Deeson cautiously shook the hand and continued, "Sir... It's kind of a jumper call, sir. He's a snowbird" Deeson jabbed his finger accusingly toward the little old man wearing a gray suit. The codger made a meek wave back at them.

"His name is Walter Hoskins. He's been a little despondent since his wife pulled through hip surgery last week." Deeson leaned in and whispered, "He hates her guts."

Bailey fought to be patient, "Okay, I get that part, what happened here?"

"Well sir, he jumped out of the third story window of the hotel and landed on the guy sitting here eating a tuna sandwich on the restaurant patio. Looks like he smashed his face right in the potato salad. It wasn't pretty. Broken arm, maybe a back injury. Concussion for sure. The amazing part is, the old geezer didn't even get a scratch."

Frank wondered if he was in Hell or the Twilight Zone. "Sarge, I hate to ask this but why did the old fart hop out of the third floor? This is a ten story hotel, he could have definitely gotten the job done if he went up a few floors."

Deeson stared up at the side of the building with the vacant expression of awed tourists when they look down the Grand canyon for the first time. "I ain't got a clue, Lieutenant."

That ain't no bullshit, Bailey mused. "More to the point Deeson, why did you call me here?"

"Skipper, the old geezer had all these pills in his pocket, there must be dozens of them." Deeson held up a clear plastic evidence bag stuffed with multi-colored pills and capsules.

"Deeson, all gum-bangers take about a hundred of those bastards a day just to have a bowel movement."

"Well, the other guy was holding a gun and a baggie with white powder stuff in it. One of the guys thought it might be cocaine or meth. We ran an NCIC check on him and he has a warrant out of Florida for drug trafficking."

Finally the moron tells me, Bailey thought. Why is getting the straight story on this job like pulling teeth? "So you're saying that a suicidal geezer did a three story half gainer and body slammed a doper, and THAT'S why I'm here?"

"Yes sir."

"Thank you sergeant, I'll have one of my detectives follow-up."

"Thanks Lieutenant, you know, I sure would like to be assigned to narcotics sometime and I'm glad I got to work with you today." Deeson whispered conspiratorially,
"It never hurts to let the boss see what you can do, right?" He gave a friendly elbow nudge to Bailey's side.

"You got that right Sergeant Deeson, I will definitely remember you when we have an opening in the Special Investigations Unit." Bailey thought he would remember to shred this idiot's application. He started to turn and leave, but as an afterthought added, "What are you going to do with Mr. Hoskins?"

"I told the guys to book him on aggravated assault, It fits... Technically."

"I tell you what Sergeant, I'd like you to write his part up in this..." Bailey waved his arm towards the scene, "Situation... as an attempted suicide and send the case to my attention, I'll take care of assigning any necessary follow up."

"You got it, Boss." Deeson, trying ineffectively to appear competent, hurried off to bother the ambulance people.

Bailey walked over to Mr. Hoskins and put his arm around him. "Sir, it appears you have just neutralized a serious threat to the quality of life in our community. My congratulations."

"Thank you, McGarret." The old man answered matter of factly.

"McGarret was Hawaii Five-o, This is Arizona. I'm Bailey."

"Huh?" The old man put a cupped hand to his ear.

"Bailey, it's Bailey."

"Barely?... I guess it was barely three stories. I should have jumped off the top of that son-of-a-bitch." The old man put his hands on his hips and stared up at the roof line of the hotel. "Where the hell is that elevator, sonny?" Hoskins started heading back for the hotel.

Bailey grabbed Hoskins by the scruff of the neck and waved over a uniformed officer he recognized. "Officer Paulson, would you please keep an eye on this gentleman?" He stage whispered as she came closer, "And no matter what, don't let him near the damned elevator."

The officer smiled at the old man who was still walking but not going anywhere, with Bailey hanging onto his collar. She put a hand on Hoskins' shoulder and directed him to the back of her patrol car."

"No worries, Lieutenant. I think I can handle this guy. He doesn't look like a dangerous man, unless maybe you're eating a tuna sandwich or something."

Bailey nodded in agreement. He walked back to his car, never looking back, and fumbled with his keys. He opened the door, sat down in the driver's seat and punched in a number on his cell phone.

The sound of Emma Flanagan's voice mail kicked in, "This is the offices of the Special Investigations Unit. If this is an emergency, hang up and dial 9-1-1, otherwise please leave a message at the tone."

Bailey kept it short. "It's after 4:00. This is Bailey. I'm heading home. I'll have my pager with me if anyone needs me."

He flipped the phone shut and whipped back into the rush hour traffic for the commute across town. He massaged the tight muscles in his neck as he drove. "I gotta learn to relax."

Bailey flipped down the sun visor and pulled on his Ray Ban Wayfarers, squinting as he drove into the afternoon sun. But while he crossed town fighting the uncomfortable brightness of sunlight, he didn't know a friend was alone, fighting the devil for his very soul.

CHAPTER 2

In spite of the glaring afternoon sun, the small apartment was dark. The air conditioner masking the Arizona heat gusted through the tiny rooms creating a chilly meat-locker effect. Always plan ahead, Joe thought. Maybe no one will show up for a few days. No sense making some young rookie puke from finding a stinker.

Joe had no pride left, but he didn't want to be found as a bloated maggot farm.

He lifted up the tail of his undershirt and wiped the perspiration from his forehead and then his hands. Shivering from cold while sweating from despair and fear, he nervously belched up a foul taste and quickly washed it down with another sip of beer.

Nothing left to do.

He picked up the phone and carefully punched in the numbers he had written on an old envelope. He waited a moment before hearing the brief message, 'I can't come to the phone right now, please leave a message and I will get back to you.' An electronic beep was Joe's cue to say good-bye.

"Frank, this is Joe. Remember me? Joe Trenton? Your old field training officer? I need to tell you something... I need to..." He began calmly, but his voice cracked as the thin thread of composure broke, "I'm so sick of this bullshit. I'm so fucking sick." He shut his eyes, forcing himself not to ramble, then he took a breath and continued, "I have a letter for you on the dresser. I'm sorry I had to leave a message like this, god-damn it." He slammed the phone down, then in silence, sat still on the kitchen chair for a few seconds with his face in his hands. Eyes tearing, he rubbed them. He rubbed harder as if trying to wipe off the indecision. Suddenly, he relaxed and dropped his hands into his lap, gesturing resignation.

He reached for his can of beer and drank one more sip before gently placing it on the table.

Joe Trenton lifted his old leather duty belt off the back of the chair. He quickly pulled his Smith and Wesson revolver out of the holster, then looked at it, inspecting it for the last time. It would need re-bluing from all the holster wear. He snorted at his own concern. Not his problem anymore.

He put his left hand on his retirement plaque, feeling the engraved sentiment: For twenty-seven years of service to the Parma City Police Department. He looked down the barrel, staring at the riflings of the muzzle, dark and cold, looking for an answer that wasn't there. Or was it? He paused.

No, not in the mouth. He placed the end of the barrel next to his temple, closed his eyes and squeezed the trigger. Involuntarily, he flinched. The .357 bullet penetrated in front of the temple and blew out through the front of his forehead. Joe's heart and lungs continued to function, but everything Joe had been on this earth making him a living soul was gone.

Seeking peace from torment, he escaped life, taking his chances with the cold blue darkness.

***

Frank walked into his apartment sensing the familiar odor of another burnt coffee pot as he passed through the door. Cursing his forgetfulness, he dashed to the kitchen to initiate damage control when he noticed the flashing light on his answering machine. He punched the play button and listened to his messages as he picked up pieces of exploded glass.

"Frank, Pete Hirosata here. There is a fight on next Saturday, pay per view, the guys are coming over. Everybody is chipping in five bucks and I'll make the chili. Stop by the restaurant this week."

A beep.

"Are you interested in an investment opportunity that can give you a 300% return..."

Frank reached up from his cleaning and hit the message advance button.

"Do you realize you are paying too much for your long distance services..."

"For crying out loud!" Thoroughly annoyed, Frank stood up and punched the advance button with his index finger, standing poised ready to terminate all sales calls with extreme prejudice.

Beep.

"Frank, this is Joe. Remember me? Joe Trenton? Your old field training officer? I need to tell you something..."

CHAPTER 3

Monday evening

Frank Bailey squeezed the limp hand one last time. Leaving a friend to die is the saddest of things. The hand still held warmth, but Frank knew that it would soon be cold and hard. He sat limply on the metal chair, leaning on his knees with his elbows, supporting his head in his hands. He lifted his head and took a deep breath then slowly looked around the tiny hospital room where his old mentor continued to breathe by means of some cold mechanical device. The room was pale green and crowded with things that, although designed for maintaining life, held an aura of malevolence. Frank frowned as he thought there was something inherently wrong with keeping the near dead alive, with no hope.

Frank had been in too many rooms like this one over the years trying to get statements out of dying victims, collecting evidence, or shooting some pictures of the trauma wrought by violent criminals. This time, he had nothing to do. Just wait for the end with a friend who would never wake up again, and by all accounts, was dead already. The repetitive sound of the ventilator caused Bailey to lose track of time.

Bailey never had been a religious person, but he believed in covering all the bases. He made an attempt at saying a prayer for a man, who had been a great cop and nothing else. Joe had no friends, save Frank, and no family left behind to mourn the loss of the best cop Frank ever knew, Big Joe Trenton. Maybe the saddest of all was the police department, the center of Joe's life, doing its best to ignore a retired cop who tried to take his own life.

Frank spoke to Joe, knowing he wouldn't be heard, "God, Joe, I hope you know I don't blame you for what you did. This world is getting so screwed up... I guess the thought even crossed my mind from time to time. You just got to know, I'll miss you. A lot of the guys you trained over the years will miss you too." Bailey next said what he consciously knew to be a lie, "You made a difference, man." Franks' eyes began to water and he stopped. My God, I'm lying to a dead man. We didn't make one damned bit of difference. He choked back a sob as he felt tears flowing freely.

"You tried. I don't know if anybody gives a shit or not, but you tried. You took the bad guys down and never looked back."

Frank fought to compose himself, quickly wiping his face as he grasped for the analytical cop side, shutting off the uncomfortable emotions. Things to do. Problems to solve. A funeral to arrange. Frank tried to concentrate. Who might grieve for this man? The Fraternal Order of Police would send a flower arrangement to the funeral. It was a standard policy. Frank couldn't remember, is Joe eligible to have the Police Honor Guard at the service, or not? Are suicides exempt from honors? The one last Christmas was a suicide and they didn't have the Honor Guard. Was it the family's request? He would have to check the manual. Assholes, he thought to himself, cursing no one in particular and the world in general.

His thoughts drifted again to the glory days as a rookie cop, cocky and out to save the world. Frank almost smiled as he remembered the euphoria. The police force, my force, filling every waking moment. Every new cop on the street believing life in the city was going to be changed for the better with them on the street. Tough cops like Frank Bailey and Big Joe making things better for the good people and Hell on criminals, but twenty years later, things are still the same. My God, what does this job do to people?

Frank stood up when the doctor came through the door. He watched as the doctor studied the displays on the machines. He forced himself to take another look at the bed holding what was left of his training officer.

Frank spoke as the doctor adjusted and checked dials and readouts on the equipment. Frank felt uncomfortable talking to the doctor, but he felt compelled to try to say something.

"Doc, I don't want to sound like some flake, but it seems like there has to be more in life, or death. I don't want to die like this, and in my heart, I can't believe Joe wanted to die like this. Joe dedicated his life to the force, the best street cop I ever knew, yet five years after retirement, he's forgotten, or worse yet, ignored as an embarrassment. There has to be more."

The doctor looked up, "I'm sorry, what was that?"

Frank ran a tissue across his nose, then pulled out a business card and handed it to the doctor, "Nothing, call me when it's over."

Lieutenant Frank Bailey, commander of the Parma City Police Department Special Investigations Unit wandered through the parking lot to his car, then he sat down behind the wheel and cried again for his dying friend and for himself. Both alone. Both with nothing. The force, their lifelong symbol of brotherhood and good, had changed and left them both behind.

***

The phone rang three times before Bailey stirred from his restless sleep. He grabbed it off the hook beating the answering machine, picking up the call by one ring.

"Yeah," was all that he could choke out, not yet fully awake. He looked at his alarm clock and saw it was 4:00 A.M.

"Frank Bailey?" A female voice asked in a formal tone.

He ran a palm over his face, cleared his throat and tried another "yeah" that came out more clearly.

The caller didn't speak right away. Bailey wondered if it was a prank call.

The voice continued after what sounded like a deep breath, "This is Mrs. Glenn from the Parma City Lutheran Hospital. I'm sorry to inform you that Mr. Joe Trenton expired at 3:45 a.m. You are listed as the next of kin and I'm afraid we'll need you here to take care of arrangements."

"Okay," Bailey responded without emotion. He had gone to bed drained and now woke up drained. He was used up. He took a deep breath and tried to respond professionally, "Please excuse me Mrs..."

"Mrs. Glenn."

"Yes, I'm sorry, Mrs. Glenn, I don't get called on to deal with things like this too often. Mr. Trenton had everything planned and written up so it should be fairly simple. There's only one additional thing he needed me to specifically take care of and I'll do that this afternoon at his former employers."

"Thank you sir, there will be an aide waiting for you at the front reception counter."

"Thank you Mrs. Glenn, I'll be there in half an hour." Bailey set the receiver down and took a sip of water from the glass on the oak night stand beside his bed before rising to face the long day ahead.

***

CHAPTER 4

Tuesday 11:00 hrs.
Parma City Police Headquarters

He expected the bureaucracy at the hospital, but now the Police Department's bean counters were pushing Frank's patience to the edge.

Bailey's face started to turn red as he spoke, "Look, the man was a retired sergeant on this police department, the badge he got when he retired was stolen several years ago. I need a new badge for his funeral service. He wanted to be buried in uniform. Why is that such a big deal?"

The Property and Supply custodian stood his ground, "I can't give you a sergeant badge just for old time's sake for your fucking pal. Those things cost $39.00 each and we don't buy them so you can bury them. Did you see a sign that said 'Goodwill' or something? Christ, it would be my ass if I gave one to you. We have policies about this you know. But you *are* a Lieutenant, and if you give me a direct order to violate the policy, I'll do it. But I want that order in writing."

Frank chewed on the inside of his cheek as he wished for a cigarette. He fantasized about pulling out his .45 and blowing this little worm's bureaucratic head off. Instead of indulging himself with the satisfaction of taking the clerk out, Frank grabbed the phone off the counter and the punched the numbers for the Captain who supervised the supply section.

"Captain, this is Frank Bailey. I need a sergeant badge for Joe Trenton's funeral. He wanted to be in uniform for the memorial service. Your man down here won't sign it out for me. Can you please cut some red tape. Hell, Joe was your friend too."

Bailey held his breath, bracing himself for disappointment.

"I thought his deal was going to have to be closed casket?" The Captain, like most cops, answered a question with a question.

"It was his request, sir. I don't know what kind of job the funeral home can do on him, but with all due respect Captain, can I please have the badge?" Frank seldom swallowed his pride, but he needed the badge.

"Frank, I tell you what I'll do. If you leave a personal check for $39.00 with the property custodian, I'll have him give you the badge, if... you promise to get it back right after the service. We can't go around burying those things. Christ, they're $39.00 apiece. I'll have the property people return your check when you return the badge, fair enough?"

"Thanks for the help Captain," Bailey replied with an acid taste in his mouth. "I'll put your man back on."

"Hey, Frank," the Captain continued before Frank could hang up, "Too bad about old Joe, but you know if a guy lets himself go to seed like that, what are you supposed to expect. He was definitely a dinosaur. Can you imagine a guy like him on the force today?"

"You mean a guy who thinks we're just here to arrest criminals?" Bailey felt his jaw tighten another notch.

"Yeah, he never got anywhere in this organization because he only focused on working the street and not paying any attention to his career. And can you imagine the embarrassment to the Department he's causing by shooting himself? I can't believe it."

Frank quit listening and handed the phone to the property custodian. He pulled his check book out of his hip pocket, scribbled out the check and grabbed the badge off the counter. Without another word to the property man, he turned and left.

Bailey stomped out of the building and got into his car. He picked up his cell phone and speed dialed the number of Sergeant Hank James, one of his few friends, and fewer confidants. Sergeant Hank James went through the academy with Bailey. He also shared the experience of having Joe Trenton for a training officer.

"Hank?"

"Yeah?"

"It's me. I'm sorry to have to call you like this, but I have some sad news to pass on. Joe Trenton passed away early this morning. He never regained consciousness."

Hank was stunned, "What happened, heart attack? Shit he was only in his early fifties."

"No... He smoked a bullet."

"Shit."

"He left a letter. I guess he had no family, he left it for me. Hell, I haven't even tried calling him for six months and he figured me to be his next of kin. I didn't know. Damn, Hank... I don't know what to think."

"There ain't nothing to think. It happens."

"I know, I just wish I could have been there for him. He was there for guys like you and me and Quintero when we were wet behind the ears baby cops, wasn't he?" Bailey paused, "Those were some good times weren't they?"

Bailey waited about thirty seconds before the reply came from his old friend. "Big Joe was the best. There aren't many more like him out there."

Bailey disagreed, "Hank, I ain't so sure there are any like him out there."

Bailey heard Hank snicker, "No shit. Things ain't like they used to be when guys like Joe were on the street. He kicked ass and never even took names. I'll sure miss that mean old son-of-a-bitch"

Frank forced a slight smile. "You could always count on the crazy bastard to do the right thing. Shit, now I don't even know what the right thing is."

Bailey lit a cigarette as his friend responded, "Yes you do, Frank. You are one of the few who still does know, or at least wants to know. What do I need to do for the service?"

"I'm not sure. I'll have to call you later after I meet with the funeral home guy."

"Let me know."

"Yeah, thanks... Hank?"

"Yeah."

"Do you think things can get any more fucked up?"

"I'll tell you this. Every man has to believe in something, and I believe that no matter how shitty things get, they can always get more fucked up."

Frank smiled, "Well, I certainly feel better now. It's good to know I can always turn to you for a few inspirational words in my times of trouble."

Bailey flipped the cell phone shut, lit the last cigarette in the pack and started his car.

CHAPTER 5

Wednesday - 3:30 A.M.

Denise Downey splashed cold water over her face from the bathroom sink. The nightmares left her blue eyes red and swollen. Being a victim is one of the hardest things for a cop to deal with. Denise wondered if the horrors she experienced as a small kid caused her choice of careers. She damned sure knew it was the cause of her nightmares.

This time the horror of her night terrors was so real and so startling she had rolled out of bed and hit her eye on the corner of the night stand in her sleep. She searched through the medicine cabinet for her little bottle of Visine and put two drops in each eye. She went through her make-up drawer to find the ingredients to hide the bruises and bags under her eyes. She paused and stared at her tired face in the mirror.

"When is this going to end?" She asked her reflection. She received only a tired stare.

She knew better than to go back to sleep. The best thing to do, she decided, was to go ahead and try to accomplish something productive. Work was better than lying in bed squirming around restlessly for the remainder of the night, consumed by the fear of having another nightmare. After all, she did get four hours sleep. That was more than usual.

Forcing herself to shake off the depressive mood, she tossed the sweat soaked University of Phoenix T-shirt she slept in into the clothes hamper with what she considered a pretty good hook shot then stepped into a hot steamy shower, followed by a blast of ice cold water. Refreshed as she could expect to be, she grabbed her robe and went into the spare bedroom and signed on to the Internet.

The Netscape menu flashed and she selected a chat room off of her bookmarks menu, 'Chicken hawk'.

The next screen gave her the discussion group for the source of her night demons. Child molesters.

Tonight's topic was the first amendment and kiddy porn, little children exploited for the sexual pleasure of perverse degenerates. Downey felt her stomach churn at the thought of the Constitution she took an oath to defend being twisted into a courtroom tool for the animals who had almost destroyed her life and were now destroying the lives of children all over the country as she sat there scanning their disgusting remarks. As she lurked in their chat room, they violated everything she had ever stood for in the name of the United States Constitution.

"You bastards."

She stopped when she saw a comment posted by a sicko calling himself Dingo. She had seen the name before. It came up on local checks from the intelligence unit. If she remembered correctly it was a moniker posted in some of the more hard-core peep shows around town.

She read his comments with revulsion.

'After eight, they're too late, give me those young ones, young boys need to learn from the master.'

She cursed again under her breath and hit the print code. She grabbed the page out of the ink jet machine and shoved it in a file folder marked 'Task Force Proposal'.

She signed off and went to the kitchen to make some coffee. Anger and stress from lack of sleep made her clumsy and she dropped her cup on the kitchen floor, sending broken pieces across the room. She sat on the floor and cried.

"That fucking animal must pay."

***

CHAPTER 6

Wednesday 11:00 A.M.

The average officer doesn't like to drive through alleys, too much chance of getting the car dirty, or worse yet, get a ding in the fender and be stuck with a mountain of accident review paperwork. Jeff Henderschott didn't give a shit about paperwork. He joined the police department to fight crime and crime isn't found in neat, tidy places. Crime is found in alleys and dark doorways, places where the bottom feeders of society can hide from the protective eyes of the police.

Henderschott picked up his plastic water bottle and gave the spray head a couple of quick squeezes sending a mist of cooling water inside the car. It was an awfully hot day to be wearing a kevlar bulletproof vest, but Jeff remembered standing with the honor guard over a dead officer who didn't think it was worth the discomfort of wearing the vest one hot Arizona summer day shift. Jeff had a towel on the seat to wipe his face. At six foot three and two-hundred and forty-five pounds, he fought a never-ending perspiration problem. It was bad enough off duty, but extremely bad when he was stuck with day shift in the summer.

His air conditioner had been blowing luke warm air since 15 minutes after the beginning of shift. He rubbed the towel over his burr haircut and said, "Come on October."

He edged the big Crown Victoria cruiser around a bend in the alley, edging past a jutting old aluminum trash can. He creeped along at about five miles per hour with his windows down. Every couple hundred feet he stopped and turned the engine off and listened for five minutes. He listened for the sound of breaking glass or the scrambling footsteps of daytime burglars, usually juveniles, who plagued the middle class neighborhood that he covered on his day shift beat.

Jeff stopped and listened as he neared his last stopping point before coming back onto the street when he heard it. A sound like an injured dog, no... small child whimpering. He stepped out of the car, gently closed the door and quietly approached the source of the sound. He placed his hand on his holstered gun out of force of habit, feeling comfort at the touch of the big Glock .45 automatic.

The officer saw a small foot protruding from behind a piece of plywood leaning against the fence. He pulled the sheet of plywood aside and stepped back startled as a nude boy about eight years old screamed liked a trapped animal. The boy's wrists and ankles were tightly bound by electrician's tape, turning his feet and hands blue from lack of circulation.

Henderschott instinctively pulled the radio off his duty belt, "Delta 505, I need an ambulance and medics at the alley between Fern and Feldon Streets, East of Baldwin Avenue, code three."

He looked down at the boy. His stomach churned as he saw obvious evidence that the child had been brutalized. Carefully, he tried not to make a sudden move that would frighten the boy more. Henderschott spoke in the softest tone he could manage, "I'm a policeman, it's okay now. I'll help you."

Jeff saw the small figure, shivering with fear, blink back a tear, then another, then burst into mournful sobs. Henderschott couldn't recall ever feeling more helpless. He lifted the radio again. "Dispatch, contact Detective Downey and ask her to meet me at the hospital. We have another one."

***

At Headquarters, Downey sat in a trance-like state, typing at the computer station she shared with five other investigators. She pounded out a proposal for a surveillance team to cover a group of local individuals involved in Internet kiddy porn. She had been developing this project over the past six months and finally felt as though she was close to going to the Chief's office with a request for manpower.

The evidence wasn't much. Her instincts told her that surveilling the suspects on the Internet lead, would yield a clue to the child molestation cases she held, cases with no leads, and unfortunately, no interest from the powers that be. She thumbed through the files again and pulled some photos. She thought the pathetic faces of her victims might stir a little action. She stopped and put the photos back in the files. "Christ, now I'm exploiting them," she mumbled to herself.

She appeared annoyed as the ringing phone broke her concentration. She stopped typing and stretched her fingers before picking up the receiver. "Detective Downey, Sex Crimes Unit... yes... Oh no, where are they taking the victim? I'll be enroute. Request the Watch Commander to secure the scene until I clear the hospital. It's what? Yeah, secure the whole alley."

She slammed the phone down and grabbed her notebook and gun. She slipped the security paddle of her Bianchi holster over her waistband and adjusted the 9 millimeter Glock 19 so it wouldn't jab her in the small of the back when she got in her car.

Downey briskly walked past the Criminal Investigation Division receptionist and said, "Lutheran Hospital" with no further explanation of her destination.

***

Downey pulled into the hospital parking lot and turned her car into the space reserved for police officers near the emergency room. She grabbed her camera and tape recorder out of the trunk and shoved them in her canvas briefcase.

The radio squawked with her call sign as she briskly walked to the entrance.

"D-5494, go ahead." She said a little breathlessly into the portable as she walked.

A male voice droned in a monotone response, "We just received a missing child report. The description matches your victim. Same general area as the victim was located."

"Check, I'll advise on land line in about five minutes."

Downey hurried by the receptionist, holding up her police ID. A nurse flagged her down to the cubicle in which the child was being treated. She saw Henderschott waiting nearby.

"Jeff, what have we got?"

Downey knew Henderschott to be a hard-ass with a stone cold poker face. His icy stare could probably stop a locomotive in its tracks with a single frosty glance, but the big patrol officer's usually tough veneer couldn't hide his emotions of disgust for the unspeakable crime he was investigating, nor his pity for the defenseless victim. Henderschott had kids of his own.

Downey noticed his eyes, red and watery. She'd known Henderschott for nine years, but never noticed him having any emotional response before, no matter how bad things were on the street. She reached up and put a hand on his shoulder.

"Jeff, are you okay?" She could hear the victim crying quietly behind the curtain as she spoke with the officer.

Henderschott's jaw muscle visibly tightened.

"Yeah, no problem."

"We might have the parents located, will you get with dispatch on the description and send mom and dad down for an ID if it matches? I want to get with the Doctor to start the examination and maybe try to talk to the victim."

"Yeah, I'll take care of it." He pulled a handkerchief out of his pocket as he walked back to the phone. He blew his nose. "Damned allergies."

Denise watched him walk off, took a deep breath, and steeled herself to do what she was trained for.

***

Seven hours later Denise finished her investigation at the hospital. She stopped at the drinking fountain to wash down a handful of aspirins.

Stepping outside she noticed that the sun was already setting. God, please let this stinking hot summer end, she thought as the sweltering heat made her clothes instantly sticky.

She got into her car and fired the engine turning the air conditioning on full blast. Denise flipped open her cell phone and called her sergeant.

"Garver," she heard the curt answer.

"Boss, it's me."

"What have you got?"

"Looks like the other two we had this past year. What have I got? Jack shit."

Garver's tone was that of a man with children, a sullen "God-damn it."

"I'm through with this for the day. The child was returned to his parents and the counselors are working with them now. I think I'll head home if you don't have anything else."

Garver was a man of few words, "See you tomorrow."

Denise flipped the phone shut and put the car in drive, fighting rush hour traffic across town to her apartment. She pulled in her parking place and fantasized about how good it would feel to pull off her pantyhose and pull on some shorts.

***

CHAPTER 7

Thursday - 11:15 A.M.

Bailey left the funeral home with the urn in his arms. He felt uncomfortable, not knowing the protocol for handling cremated dead friends. Should he carry the urn in front of him with both hands, or tuck it under his arm like a football? Shit.

He used what he decided was the more dignified approach until he was out of view of the undertakers, then he carried Joe by one handle and tossed him on the front seat of the car.

"Sorry pal."

He drove to another retired cop's house and banged on the door. A portly man with a mop of curly white hair, wearing baggy jeans, a white T-shirt and red suspenders answered with a grin. The man extending a big paw of a hand. "Hi Frank, how the hell have you been?"

"I'm okay, Kingfish. Things are as good as can be expected, considering..." Bailey shrugged towards the car.

"Shit, is he... in the car?" Claude 'Kingfish' Boyer took a step back and peeked out the door like a boogie man might be waiting for him.

"'Fraid so. Feels weird," Bailey confided, peeking cautiously over his shoulder, feeding off the case of the creeps from Kingfish.

Kingfish stared wide-eyed at the car, "Damn!"

"Look Fish, I mentioned to you about Joe wanting his ashes spread on the lake, and I guess I'm the one responsible for doing it. Is it still okay if I borrow your pick-up and boat for a couple of days to go over to Lake Havasu and take care of this?"

Fish looked nervous enough at the thought of a dead guy in his driveway, Frank thought, he would probably give him anything he asked for to get rid of them.

"Sure Frank, Joe was a good friend, no problem." He peeked again. "Damn."

He handed the keys to Frank.

Frank thanked him and parked his car on the street before hitching up the boat, tossing Joe in the truck bed on an old army blanket, and heading West on Interstate 10 for the four hour drive to Lake Havasu.

***

The little outboard on the small aluminum bass boat pushed Frank slowly toward the middle of the lake. Looking back, he could see the bridge spanning the small channel near the tourist area of Lake Havasu City, a small town built around the dark blue man-made lake and the original London Bridge.

Frank found what seemed to be an appropriate spot and stopped the boat. He bobbed gently, enjoying the smell of the lake water and the unique blue color of Lake Havasu. He lit a cigarette and enjoyed the smoke as he relaxed.

He reached into the cooler and pulled out a cold can of Coors beer. He popped the cap and lifted it in the direction of the urn. "Here's to the boat trip we talked about for twenty years and never got around to taking. We were always to busy. Too busy pissing our lives away for a losing cause. Now it's..." He felt his eyes welling with tears and an involuntary sob burst from his lungs. Tears flowed in the little boat as Frank cried for Joe and for himself.

Frank stopped as suddenly as he started, feeling embarrassed at the emotional outburst.

He took a deep breath. "Fuck it." He pulled off the lid of the urn and emptied Joe's remains over the side, then stood up and tossed the urn out into the water. He watched sadly as his friend sank to the bottom of the lake. Another sacrifice to the cold blue darkness. Another officer down, for eternity.

He lit a second cigarette off the first one before tossing the glowing butt into the water and turning the little boat back towards shore.

CHAPTER 8

Monday morning
Special Investigations Unit (SIU) Offices

Bailey centered the police department memo on his desk. Elbows touching each edge of the white paper, hands grasping his head at the edges of his eyes to steady his vision, he remained motionless. His eyes shifted once, from his ash tray to the memo. Unmoving, he continued staring, not reading anymore, just staring, for another five full minutes. He blinked... then blinked again, and his face contorted. He slammed his palms down on the desk, and threw his head back, grimacing in agony. Just as suddenly, he grabbed the memo, wadded it up and threw it on the floor in front of his desk. "Fucking Commie environmentalist assholes. I hope they rot in Hell for this bullshit. When they let that asshole consumer rights guy get rid of the Corvairs, I knew shit like this would happen. Those democrat tree hugging bastards!" He kicked over his government wastebasket and threw his government stapler across the room.

His administrative assistant, Emma Flanagan, came around to the front of her desk and waited outside his office when the burst of profanity exploded from the room. Cussing a blue streak wasn't very unusual, but when the cacophony escalated to include the slamming of file drawers, the throwing of staplers and the wholesale destruction of various office supplies, it could only mean a full blown Bailey tantrum was in progress.

In this type of situation, most of the administrative assistants at the police department would run for reinforcements, but not Emma. Like a medic at a crash scene, she quickly dug into the huge sea bag she called a purse and pulled out a couple of little airline liquor bottles. A hint of a naughty Irish smile appeared at the corner of her mouth. Time for 'Mutha' to step in, she thought.

Compared to a lot of bosses Emma had in the past, Bailey was usually a pretty quiet guy, but he was known to throw a fit once in a while. Emma figured supervising over fifty undercover cops was reason enough to justify an occasional childish outburst from Mother Theresa, let alone a mere mortal like Lieutenant Bailey. His mood swings had been a little more extreme since Joe Trenton committed suicide, but the boss was a rock. She opened his office door, stuck her head in, and gave him that look. The 'Okay you had your tantrum now what's wrong' look.

"What's the problem, Franky, is it that time of the month?" She leaned against the door jam and held the little liquor bottles behind her back.

Bailey looked up at the tall, full-figured red head, "Oh blow it out your ass, you horrible woman. We never had these problems before you people got the vote."

Emma tried to look mad but she wanted to laugh. She knew nobody else in the department ever did as much to support the cause of women entering the "boys' club" of police work, but the boss always enjoyed acting the part of a backward, fascist, oppressor of women and minorities.

"I'll get you some prozac for your cup of coffee, honey. You just calm down." She unscrewed the cap off the little bottle and poured a shot of vodka in his favorite coffee cup, the black one bearing a yellow happy face emblem with a bullet hole in its forehead.

"Did you see this shit?" He pointed a shaking finger at the crumpled memo on the floor. He grabbed his cup, slurped some of Emma's special blend coffee, then sat sideways in his chair pouting.

Emma's expression changed to concern. This looked serious. "No, what is it?" Her voice softened as she kneeled to pick the memo up and uncrumple it.

"All public buildings in the city are now designated 'non-smoking areas' and all Division Commanders are required to enforce it."

Her red face matched her red hair, "THOSE BASTARDS! Those testosterone- infested Republican nazi scumbags can't do this. This is Bullshit!"

It was the boss's turn to do damage control. Bailey tried to soothe her with calming words, "Welcome to the fucking nineties."

"I quit smoking seven times last year! What do those bastards want?" She shrieked. "I'll put on a hundred pounds, I just know it." Attempting to maintain the facade for her ideal of equality in a man's world, she put her hand to her face to conceal her trembling lower lip, "I'm going to lunch!" She grabbed a box of tissues and her purse and stomped off to the women's restroom fighting tears of rage.

Bailey was alone in the office. He spoke towards Emma's empty desk. "Well please copy and post this memo in the offices on your way out. Thank you."

He sat quietly for a minute, then his lower lip started trembling. "Screw it, I'm going to lunch." He grabbed his .45 and stuffed it in the back of his waistband, scrounged through his lap drawer and the office chairs to find enough change for a cup of coffee, and left the building to pout in peace.

***

Bailey came back from his early lunch to review completed drug buy cases and to work on the quarterly report. He sat at his desk reading.

"Shit, I left my glasses at home." He said to himself as he rubbed his eyes and squirmed in his chair.

Bailey continued reading and fidgeting, reaching toward his shirt pocket every fifteen seconds or so for a smoke, then pulling back empty handed.

After about ten minutes, he rubbed his eyes again, "This reading without glasses is bullshit, I think I'll take a little walk."

This time he pulled the pack of smokes out of his pocket and messed with them as he entered the hallway, counting them and examining the condition of the pack. He looked up to see all the smokers in the unit in a state of transit, either walking to or from the elevators taking smoke breaks.

He started to say something to them, but looked back at his own pack of cigarettes and decided maybe he'd get them all together later for a unit pep talk. He needed to get outside. Damned glasses.

Tuesday - Day shift

While cruising down Main Street, Frank listened to a Johnny Cash song on the radio about a guy getting ripped off by an ex-wife. Bailey made a conscious choice to be in a bad mood. He wasn't any happier today than when he drove to work yesterday. Bailey tried to sing along in his best baritone but couldn't recall any of the words. He pushed in the cigarette lighter. Thank God the smoking ban hadn't spread to company vehicles yet. Bailey knew a loophole for that eventuality anyway. The SIU cars weren't owned by the city, they were leased from a car rental company so narcs and other covert operators in SIU could change cars whenever they took a 'burn'. The thought of a legal loophole finally working in his favor for a change made Bailey smile as the lighter popped and he touched it to the tip of the cigarette. The next to the last one in his last pack. He felt around the crack of the car seat to see if there was enough loose change to pick up a fresh pack.

Downtown traffic was unusually bad. "Another shitty day in la-la-land," Bailey cursed as he drove around the block for the third time in fifteen minutes, trying to find a parking space that might save him a one-hundred foot walk. The buzzing vibration coming from his waistband caused him to curse under his breath as he punched the button on his pager for the fifth time since he got in his car to go to work. "Another friggin' 9-1-1 page. Screw it. I ain't calling anybody back until I get a cup of coffee." He punched the button twice and cleared all messages.

He spotted an open parking space on the street outside their building and whipped the leased Taurus into the parallel slot like a parking valet at the Hilton. He grabbed his black ballistic nylon bag of guns, radios, and paperwork and got out of the car. He trudged across the parking lot to the steps of his office building, the third floor of which was the home of the

Special Investigations Unit. For security purposes the third floor was advertised on the lobby register under the false front of Sal's Cargo and Transit.

An old bum loitered near the entrance. He wore a sleeveless army fatigue shirt and orange swimming trunks. The transient ranted about something to do with the government as he handed out little slips of paper. Bailey tried to make out the crude scrawling on the cardboard sign the man had strung around his dirty neck. 'Agent Orange -Vietnam Vet'. The transient approached Bailey on the steps of the office building, cutting him off from the entrance doors.

"Can I have your spare change, sir... For a disabled vet?" He stuck his hand out in Bailey's chest and burped the unmistakable essence of Thunderbird wine and marijuana breath in the Lieutenant's face.

At a closer glance Bailey realized the bum wasn't old, just dirty, and he damned sure wasn't old enough to be a Viet Nam vet.

"Sorry Agent Orange, I think you're going to have to go hump somebody else's leg," Bailey told him without slowing.

The bum gave him the finger. "You Fascist asshole," he shouted as Bailey entered the lobby of the building.

Bailey didn't look back. "I never been called that before...coffee this morning," he mumbled to himself as he waited for the elevator in the lobby.

Lieutenant Bailey found his SIU administration offices empty. He looked around the room. "Where the hell is everybody?"

Bailey noticed that Emma's things were missing off her desk. He tossed his gear bag on the old couch in his office and walked down to the cubicles occupied by the intelligence unit, final burial ground of old, burned out narcs. That office was empty too.

Bailey's vacant expression degraded to concern. Was the whole day shift crew AWOL? He placed his hands on his hips and looked around. Where the hell was everybody? It crossed his mind that maybe he better check those pages. They actually might have been important this time.

He walked back down the hall towards his office when he smelled it, cigarette smoke. He turned back down the hall to the elevators and did a tactical quick peak around the corner, catching a glimpse of the little six foot by six foot fire escape landing, the floor's only designated smoking area. The door was propped slightly open with a pepper spray canister.

A billowing cloud of cigarette smoke rolled through the doorway and into the hall. Bailey investigated. He peered through the doorway. In the smoky haze he made out what appeared to be human figures. Emma, four old intelligence unit investigators, an analyst, and another secretary were squashed into the confined area of the fire escape landing. They were working off a notebook computer, an old typewriter (God knows where they found that antique), and several cellular phones. Numerous styrofoam cups of coffee were dispersed throughout the jumbled mess with one or two boxes of Dunkin' Donuts'.

Bailey held the door open, staring in disbelief at the mess. "What the..."

The group raised their coffee cups in a sheepish toast to the boss. A detective weakly offered, "It's a Maxwell House moment, Skipper."

Bailey gave him a lethal stare.

Emma stood up and handed Bailey a cup of coffee and a donut, "Here's your breakfast, Hon."

The intelligence analyst interrupted, "Maybe the boss would prefer decaf? He seems a little tense."

Emma ignored him and took the offensive on Bailey, "We've been paging you all morning. Where have you been?"

"Where have I been? Well, I guess I screwed up and went to the wrong office." He put his hand on his pager, "Are all those 9-1-1 calls I got on the way to work from those cellulars?" He pointed to the small bank of cell phones laying on the floor.

"Yeah, we forgot the creamers and we were going to have you pick some up at the coffee shop in the lobby."

"I guess I really did screw up," Bailey reached for a smoke.

"Here's your chair, Boss," one of the Intel guys handed Bailey a folded lawn chair. Bailey took it, wondering whose front yard they stole it from. He decided not to ask.

"Thanks," Bailey sat down with his troops. He had heard a slogan somewhere about 'if the government outlaws cigarettes, only outlaws will have them ...' or something like that. It made him feel a little like George Washington. He lit up a Lucky Strike he bummed off one of the detectives and went to work.

***

Downey carried an armload of files as she walked from the briefing room to her desk. Her sergeant, Tom Garver, passed her in the hallway, then turned and called to her, "Denise, remember, you have mandatory cultural sensitivity training this afternoon at personnel."

Downey stopped and turned, "Sarge, I'm buried here. I have mandatory crime to fight." She gave the middle aged supervisor a look of frustration.

The sergeant gave her the disinterested shrug all sergeants use when an officer starts whining. "I know Denise, everybody in the unit is buried, but this class is mandatory. Every city employee is scheduled to attend and supervisors are under orders from the Chief to write up anybody who doesn't show."

"Sarge, this is bullshit, I have three open molest cases here, a task force proposal to write, and a kiddy porn investigation waiting for me. I never had a complaint in my life about cultural sensitivity. I'm as sensitive as any of these other assholes on the department."

Garver massaged his temple with his hand. "Downey, I'm busy too. And I not only have to make you go to the son-of-a-bitching class, I have to go to the damned thing myself. I even have to act like I give a shit. Don't even start this crap with me, Downey. Just be there."

Downey realized she had pushed the envelope on acceptable levels of whining. "Yes, sir. Sorry."

Sergeant Garver was already walking away, "I'm sorry too, Denise. Just be there."

Downey walked back to her cubicle. She adjusted her skirt and took off her jacket before sitting at her desk. She sorted through the stack of manila files and began making notes on what action she could take today, or at least this morning.

She stopped and set down her pen and pulled a small mirror out of her purse. She glanced around the office to make sure no one would catch her acting like a woman. She gave herself a hard look in the little compact glass. At age thirty-two she could pass for mid-twenties easily. She looked at the scar at the corner of her left eye. Everyone told her it wasn't even noticeable but to her, it stood out and screamed to the world that Downey was a victim. She tolerated abuse. She tolerated it as a child and tolerated it as a grown woman from a drug abusing punk of an ex-husband. She saw her eyes harden.

My God woman, she thought as she quickly stuffed the mirror back in the purse, let that garbage go.

She pulled a tissue out of the box on her desk and dabbed at the corner of her eyes.

Damn, I'm losing my sense of humor. She decided to treat herself to a call on the department's Watts line to her mom in Austin later that morning, and maybe, just maybe she could squeeze in a little time with Frank this week. It had been a while. Things hadn't been right since his friend died.

***

SIU Office

Emma threw the last of her paperwork in the bottom drawer of her desk. She looked at the wall clock above the entrance door to the SIU offices and smiled at the big hand on twelve and the little one on five. Miller time. She hit the speed dial button on her phone and rang Downey's cell phone.

She listened for a moment and then "Hello."

She smiled her Irish bomb thrower smile, "Hey dear, get your skinny butt over to Garcia's for a margarita. I got some of the gang reporting there for happy hour and we'd all love to see your shining little face."

"I don't know Emma. I'm pretty wasted. I had to go to cultural sensitivity training today."

"Oh, you poor baby! How was it?" Emma said in a sing-song voice, knowing full well what the response would be.

"It sucked. I'd like to kill the ignorant son-of-a-bitch who thought that class up."

Emma laughed, "That bad, huh?"

"Sensitivity sucks. The only good thing about the class was Sergeant James. He got pissed off when the guy started telling him how black people felt about cops so he got up and made some speech about how he was black and nobody ever asked him how he was supposed to feel about the police. Then he spouted off about how his son was a Marine... You know how he sticks *that* in every conversation. Needless to say, all the cops in the class started hooting and cheering. It was kind of funny, a bunch of Black, Asian, Hispanic, you-name-it American mutt cops all yelling and rowdy. You couldn't help but feel kind of patriotic. Then Hank shook his fist and called the facilitator a fucking communist. The facilitator got so mad I thought he was going to call Sarge the infamous 'N' word. James told the guy, let me be sure to get this right, he was a 'Draft dodging, Hanoi Jane loving, liberal pussy', or something to that effect. They kept calling each other names and started shoving when a couple of big motor cops finally jumped in and pulled them apart before they came to blows. The sensitivity consultant stomped off cussing and giving us the finger. Some guy from personnel had to come in and finish the class."

 Emma threw her head back, laughing as she spun her chair around. "I could see Hank telling off those pompous assholes. I think I'll page him and get him to come over for a drink. I believe he'll need it."

 Denise softened her voice, "Emma, will Frank be there?"

 "I don't know, sweetie. He has been spending a lot of time alone lately. I worry about him. He hasn't been the same since Joe checked out. I don't think he'll show."

 "Okay. Maybe I better just go home too. I had a really bad day. I think maybe I better head home and try to get some rest. I'm just not up to any fun tonight."

 "I understand, honey. Call me tomorrow."

 "Will do."

 Emma paged Hank while thinking about her two chronic psychiatric patients, Frank and Denise.

I wish those two would get together and get out of this rat hole. Maybe they would be people again.

The phone rang and she went back to work on the happy hour schedule.

CHAPTER 9

Wednesday - Day shift

Lieutenant Frank Bailey, leaned back in the brown government-issue office chair and propped his feet on his desk. He felt in his shirt pocket for a cigarette. Life hadn't been the same at the Special Investigations Unit since the building went "smoking free". With all the fresh air to breathe his detectives and staff had more energy to gain weight, get irritable, and make his life miserable.

He peered over the top of his cluttered desk at the cop sitting across the room. Bailey knew he wasn't the typical candy ass undercover cop who runs out and gets a tattoo and an earring the first day on the job. This guy was the real thing.

The man looked as if he weighed in at about two-hundred and sixty pounds. His long beard had breakfast, lunch, and possibly happy hour debris in it, mixed liberally with chewing tobacco and spittle. His hands and arms looked as though he just changed the oil on a semi-truck. His issue weapon was stuffed in his hip pocket. He didn't waste belt space for a radio or handcuffs, not that there wasn't ample space available. He just didn't need them. Bailey recalled overhearing him tell a rookie that backup was for wimps, and an unconscious prisoner doesn't need to be cuffed. A cigarette dangled from the corner of his mouth, unlit.

They stared each other down for a pregnant minute, unmoving, as if in a trance.

Bailey made the first move. The commander pulled a smoke out of his pack and just held it in his hand. There wasn't a regulation against just holding one. He looked at the generic convenient-mart brand cigarette. He used to smoke Marlboros, until his second ex-wife wiped him out financially.

"What's the story, Snort? I got a call indicating you were involved in that in-custody death situation last night." Bailey realized that he had been calling this man by his street name for so long, he had forgotten the detective's real name.

"Shit boss, you heard about that already? It wasn't anything."

"Well, it must have been something. The Captain called my sorry ass up first thing this morning and he wants a full briefing. Is the guy dead or what?" He rolled the cigarette in his hand.

"Yeah, I sat on him, and later he died." The undercover cop tried a facial expression of angel-like innocence and rolled his eyes slightly up, and to the left. It didn't help. He still looked like he just murdered his parents.

"Well did you sit on his head, or what? Christ, the guy really died?"

"It sounds worse than it is, Skipper. I rolled up on a typical 'psycho causing a disturbance' call. A bunch of uniforms were trying to cuff this guy but they couldn't hold him, so I walked over and sat on his butt and they cuffed him." Snort played with his lighter, increasing the level of torment.

Flick... snap... flick... snap.... flick... snap.. Bailey felt the urge to scream.

The Lieutenant put his hand up like a traffic officer trying to block the lighter from his vision. "Look, I realize holding a guy down with your butt isn't fatal, but you shouldn't have gotten involved. They're going to say you sat on his head and that's what killed him. You know that's how these things always go. Didn't you ever hear of Rodney Fucking King, for Christ sake?"

"Hell, yes. But I got photos. I told you I only sat on his butt." flick.... snap.... flick... snap...

The boss could feel a twitch developing in the corner of his left eye, "What do you mean, you got photos? Did you have the ID section take a trophy shot for you?" Bailey felt the acid churning in his stomach again.

"Hell no, Skipper. The newspaper photographer was there, and he took the picture. I ain't stupid." Flick...snap...flick...snap...

Bailey swung his feet to the floor and leaned forward. "A newspaper photographer? Jesus H. Christ. Give me that thing, god-damn it!" He reached across the desk and grabbed the lighter out of the narc's hand, jammed the cigarette into his mouth, and lit it. He puffed with grim determination until his blood pressure subsided to stroke level. "Are you saying the media was there?"

"Yes sir, he got the whole thing on film." Snort smiled confidently as he watched his boss light another generic brand smoke off the first one, "He said it was cool and was going to send me a copy of the shots. Do you want a copy?"

"Look, just how did this loser croak off?" Realization crept into the tobacco clouded mind of Bailey long enough for him to figure out he was being fucked with.

Bailey's best guess on this scam was that the other morons in the unit sent Snort in to make the boss break the 'no-smoking rule' first, so they could light up and get back to business as usual. He knew he'd been had.

Snort took his time and gracefully as Barishnikov, lit up a camel non-filter. He took a long drag and exhaled. "The medical examiner says it's a clear case of cocaine overdose. All I really did was sit on his butt and then later he died. José was the guy from the paper. He gave me the negative and a print. Snort pulled an 8 X 10 glossy out of his sleeveless denim jacket and threw it on Bailey's desk.

The Lieutenant picked it up and looked at the shot of Snort sitting on the suspect's legs, while some uniforms were cuffing the struggling coke head. Snort's back was to the photographer and his disgusting white, pimply buttocks was amply displayed between his sagging jeans and the bottom of his T-shirt. The picture was autographed, "To Lieutenant Bailey; Crack kills, Love Snort."

Snort got up and headed for the door, "Enjoy the smoke, Skipper."

Bailey yelled at his departing detective, "You're fired asshole!" He took a long drag, exhaled with a satisfied smile, then muttered to himself, "I should have joined the fucking fire department." He began rooting through his bottom drawer for a picture frame.

***

General Investigations Division
Headquarters

Downey stood by the printer, observing her recommendation slowly churn out page by page. She sorted through the report by hand ignoring the noise and confusion of the clerical work stations in the big administrative office. Denise proofread through the report, cursing and making marks with a red pen when she found errors.

***

Across the room, Celia Carpenter, a nineteen year old clerk watched Downey shuffling the papers. Downey was her hero, a woman that didn't take any shit and still looked like a super model.

Celia wanted to go to the academy someday but she didn't have a real burning desire to put on a uniform and work the street. She just wanted to be a detective like Downey. Somebody all the guys talked about. She remembered when Downey had been in uniform working a beat where Celia lived in the projects.

Celia remembered Downey sitting down and talking with her one time in the coffee room, telling war stories. Denise told her about being a beat cop for six years before becoming a detective and how tough it was for a slender blonde haired woman to work in the projects as an officer.

Downey laughed when Celia told her she was raised in that neighborhood and remembered Denise being a cop there when she was a little girl. Everybody in the 'hood' thought Downey was a hard-ass who never cut anybody any slack. But Celia added that the kids in the neighborhood said that about all the cops who were good.

Celia watched Downey bend over to pick up a piece of paper she dropped. She admired Downey's physical attributes too. She thought to herself, If I had legs and a butt like that, I'd have me a Captain for a husband before you could say J. Edgar Hoover wears a tutu.

Celia wanted to be like Downey but she preferred to avoid the kind of scary stuff that happens in the patrol division. Dealing with assholes and irate 'good' citizens.

Celia sighed and went back to work at her desk, transcribing investigative interview tapes. She thought, If I just lose another 64 pounds, I think I can pass that physical test to be an officer, and then, look out.

She took another bite of her frosted cinnamon bun while she adjusted her earphones.

Garvers's Office

Denise gave the proposal for the task force operation on her child molestation cases to Sergeant Garver. He thumbed through the twenty-odd pages of statistics and costs, reviewing the highlights of what Downey proposed.

"This is quite an operation, Denise."

"Molesting kids is quite a crime, Sarge." She responded with her toothpaste commercial smile that usually enabled her to get her way.

"You want the Special Investigations Unit to place a list of 10 known molesters, who you identified as local perverts off an Internet chat line, under surveillance while another group of 8 detectives go door to door in the areas of occurrence looking for leads. That's quite a bit of manpower for so few open cases."

"I know. But my thoughts are that if the Special Investigations Unit spends a day or two on each suspect gathering intelligence on things like their vehicles, associates, and hang-outs, we might be able to couple that in with the door to door operation to shake loose a lead. Otherwise, a sexual predator is running around town and I got nothing to do but wait for another victim who might be more help, or worse yet, may have enough physical evidence on their dead body for the lab to do something. I just think for a week or two of work, it would be worth it."

"You know they'll ask why we aren't just doing it ourselves here in sex crimes."

"Sarge, just tell them. We can't even keep up with filing the paperwork for the cases on the losers patrol arrests let alone go out and really investigate our open cases properly."

"Denise, I got a better idea. I'll let you tell them. I'll try to schedule you to present your request in front of the command staff tomorrow morning. You up to it?"

"Hell yes, Sarge, as long as you'll go with me. I need somebody to grab me if my Texas attitude kicks in." Denise gave a relaxed smile.

"No worries, Downey." He pulled his expandable baton out of his hip pocket and pointed it at her feigning a threat, "You start to lose it in front of that bunch of bureaucrats and I'll smack you up the side of the head with my Kerrigan tool. Guaranteed to adjust attitudes of ice skaters and snotty young detectives."

She laughed, "I guess I'll just force myself to be courteous and lady-like."

"Yeah, try that. I'd like to see it just once before I retire." He returned the proposal to her. "Get ten copies made, one for each Captain and Chief."

Denise took the papers and started to leave. She stopped and turned in the doorway. "Thanks boss. I mean it, this one is important to me."

Sergeant Garver didn't look up. "Ten copies, Denise."

CHAPTER 10

Outside the Chief's office

His stomach growled and flip-flopped from the moment he received the phone call directing him to report to the Chief's office. The handful of antacid tablets Bailey gobbled down were no match for the gushes of stomach acid which accompany such a call.

Bailey's mind raced as he tried to predict what trouble he was in this time. His hands stuffed in his pockets, he nervously paced outside the Chief's inner sanctum.

I hate going in that arrogant bastard's office, he thought, recalling the last time he was dragged in there for an ass-chewing. Frank had seen aircraft carriers with a smaller landing surface than the Chief's desk. He figured since the Chief was such a pussy, he needed a big desk to hide behind.

Bailey guessed it had to have something to do with the cigarette thing. Ever since the Chief had that heart attack, or whatever it was, life had been hell for red meat eating, beer drinking, cigarette smoking cops. Then again, maybe the boss was still pissed about the time he caught Bailey's undercover guys burping the Pledge of Allegiance at the Academy?

Waiting was always the hard part. Chief Lyle "Milquetoast" Milton was famous for having his secretary park your butt in front of her desk while he waited somewhere, probably in a coffin, until you were totally scared shitless. Then he liked to make an entrance and just plain mind-fuck you. Bailey looked around, nobody would notice if I just touched a cigarette.

Just as that fiendish thought crossed his mind a shadow crossed the doorway. Bailey flinched, "Ah shit."

"I beg your pardon, Lieutenant?"

"Excuse me sir, I said 'that's it', I was just trying to remember the UCR code for trespassing and I remembered just now."

"Well what was it?" The Chief's tone of voice always seemed as friendly as the stuff you pour into the toilet to dissolve the brown stains. It had that 'I'm dissolving shit right now, but if you sit here before I'm through, I'll dissolve your butt' sound of impending doom.

"What was what?"

"What was the code, Lieutenant," Milquetoast pompously hitched his trousers up as he walked back into the officer to his leather chair, crossed his arms, and plopped himself down.

Bailey blankly stared at the Chief as if the question was phrased in Chinese. A loud chirp of Bailey's cellular phone broke the silence.

Bailey flipped the cellular open and followed Milton's path from the reception area to the office where he sat in the chair the chief pointed him towards. Milton leaned back in the giant executive chair behind his desk, staring impatiently at the ceiling.

"Yeah," Bailey spoke into the mouthpiece having no idea who to expect on the other end. He listened for a moment, stood up and walked across the room. Bailey nodded his head and made two theatric glances to the Chief. The Chief began to look concerned.

Bailey nodded again and said, "I can be there in five minutes if the troops need me." Another pause, "Well wait, the Chief needs me here to talk about something," He looked up at Milton with puppy dog eyes.

The Chief leaned further up in his chair. Nervously, he reached for a pen, although he had nothing to write down.

Bailey continued on the phone, a grim frown crossing his face "Do you think this involves kids?... Maybe gang activity?... Look, I'm sorry, I can't break loose at the moment. The Chief needs me here right now..."

Milton stood up again, and waved his hands like an umpire calling a runner safe. "No, no, no... Go on... This can wait... The streets come first."

Bailey tried to appear disappointed as he put his hand over the phone and answered the boss, "I'm terribly sorry sir... I'll get back as quickly as I can."

"Whatever, Frank... Just take care of this thing, and by all means, good luck." Milton gave his little fake wink and nod that was supposed to tell the officers, 'I'm one of you guys', but it really meant, 'I hope the public thinks I'm one of you meatheads.'

Bailey escaped into the hall and left the administration section at a fast walk. He jogged down the stairs to the parking lot and finished the cigarette he had lit as he hit the exit door.

"Damn that was close." He lit another smoke and waited.

A blue Nissan with dark tinted windows pulled up beside him and he heard the sound of power door locks. He opened the passenger door and leaned inside.

"Thanks, Denise. I owe you."

The leggy blonde in the Nissan smiled with what looked like two thousand white, shiny teeth that almost took Bailey's mind off her short skirt. She struck a sexy pose, leaning back in the seat with her arms stretched in such a way as to cause openings between the buttons of her silk blouse, not enough that a guy could see anything, but enough to make him wish he could. Detective Denise Downey spoke in her soft, Texas accent that she usually tried to suppress around everyone but her closest friends, "I saw you dragging your sorry ass into Milquetoast's office, so I thought I had better call your cellular phone and give you a chance to scram out of there." She gave him a sexy wink that made his knees weak, "Tell me something, Mister Frank Bailey, how do you manage to keep a straight face when I'm giving you that great phone sex anyway? Don't you like my type anymore?"

"Babe, I lust for you in all my dreams, but just one look at Milquetoast and boom, limp noodle city. Posters of that bonehead could curb world overpopulation."

"Then maybe you better come over to my place this afternoon and pay me back for rescuing you."

"Sorry Denise, my ass is exhausted and I got about another four hours work ahead of me. How about Wednesday?"

"How about four hours from now. I'll draw a nice hot bath and ice down some white wine. Just what a tired old body like yours needs. I got some good news today and feel like celebrating. And you know how I like to celebrate." She seductively ran her palm across her thigh.

Bailey knew he was had, and happy at the prospect. "Oh shit... Let me think about it... I could go home and have a

Keystone beer and finish my can of Spaghetti-o's. And I do have a tape of Rio Bravo to watch.... Or I could spend the evening with..." Bailey looked her over again, unable to find the words to describe her. "What should I do? Decisions.... Decisions." He stepped back from the car and held his hands out in a gesture of surrender, a 'possum eating shit grin' on his face.

"Be there or be castrated, chauvinist!" Denise laughed. He slammed the car door shut and she sped away.

Bailey tried to think about baseball as he crossed the parking lot and got into his car. After a few minutes he felt his hormones subside to a level low enough to permit him to safely drive toward the SIU office. Still smiling as he left the police complex, he thought, it's nice to be appreciated by somebody, particularly somebody like Denise. What she sees in a beat up has-been like me, I'll never understand. Maybe I can get that quarterly report done in three hours.

Bailey wheeled into the entrance of the parking garage closest to the offices leased by the undercover units. As he pulled through the entrance he saw six of his SIU people running after a pair of long haired, heavily tattooed, dirty white men. The man in the lead had a brown paper bag in one hand and a gun in the other. Bailey jammed his brakes and watched wide-eyed as the undercover cops drew their guns and howling a cacophony of verbal commands at the suspects as they ran," DROP THE -..LAY ON THE -.... PUT UP YOUR-..." interspersed with profanities and curses. Bailey looked to his left to see Snort clearing a corner and running like a ruptured grizzly bear at a distant ninth place, screaming something to the effect of 'Slow down you assholes'.

Bailey fought the normal cop instinct to get out of the car and run with the herd. Squealing tires, he pulled his car through the garage, exited the other end, and made a sharp turn to the right in a calculated chance to head them off at the pass.

As he whipped the wheel blindly around the corner he came face to face with one of the suspects flying over the hood of his car, as the long haired bandit's nose smashed against the windshield.

"Shit." He instinctively slammed his brakes and threw his arms in front of his face. The suspect rolled off the drivers side of the car and lay as still as a slab of dead meat.

Bailey threw the car in park and looked around, considering just going home. His mind scrambled through possibilities. Who would have seen me? Who might have seen my plate? Shit! He took a deep breath and settled down. He got out of the car and leaned over the motionless figure, gulped and checked for a pulse.

The figure suddenly sprang to an upright position like a vampire sitting up in a casket, causing Bailey to fall backwards gasping in shock. Eyes bulging, the man screamed in Bailey's face "You gotta help me get out of here man, the cops are on my ass!"

Bailey reflexively slugged him in the chin with a left uppercut rendering the bug-eyed man unconscious once again.

"Shit, I hope nobody saw that," the Lieutenant muttered as he looked around the area for witnesses again.

Bailey's police instincts took over. Call back-up. He got up and walked over to his car massaging his sore left hand. He threw open the drivers side door and searched under the front seat, emptied the glove box and sorted through the trash pile of fast food wrappers and empty styrofoam coffee cups behind the front seat. Unsuccessful in the interior, he stepped around to the trunk and rummaged through his equipment bags until he found his radio.

"Adam 3233 to any SIU unit, I have a suspect in custody...Shit, the battery's dead." He rummaged around the car some more but was unable to find his spare battery. "Screw it," He stood on the roof of his car and shouted for help.

Within seconds one of the guys came around the corner, "Hey, you got one, Skipper....cool!"

Bailey looked down at a little scrawny surfer-looking narc wearing baggy Bermuda shorts and a tank top with a Glock 26 in his hand and a badge on a metal chain dangling from his neck. "Where are the other guys?"

The surfer narc looked alarmed, he wasn't expecting a quiz. "I don't know, I got lost."

Bailey shook his head as he hopped down off his car roof. He thought he'd probably have to add a line to the SIU manual indicating the importance of everyone holding hands during field trips.

"Do you have any cuffs?"

"No." The narc looked up at the sky hoping for a better answer.

"Why the hell not?" Bailey asked, hoping the young undercover cop wouldn't ask where Bailey's cuffs were.

"I don't know... Snort says cuffs are for pussies."

Bailey cursed to himself. "How about a radio?"

"Yeah." The young narc nodded enthusiastically after finally giving a good answer. He pulled a portable radio out of his hip pocket and proudly showed it to Bailey.

Bailey suddenly pictured the time his golden retriever proudly placed a partially decomposed gopher at his feet. Proud but clueless.

"Well, call for help for crying out loud and let's get this dirtbag to jail!"

"You got it, Skipper....What's he arrested for?"

Bailey felt a knot in his stomach. "I don't know. Why were you assholes chasing him?"

"I don't know, I was chasing him because Snort was chasing him."

"Shit." Bailey ran his hand through his thinning hairline. "See if you can find out what we want this guy for before he comes to again."

"Again?"

"Just do it, god-damn it!" Bailey turned and spit on the ground. He reached for his smokes, got another generic brand cigarette out and lit it. Feeling guilty, he stuck one in the suspect's mouth for when he woke up again. If this guy didn't do anything, then a little generosity might look good for the law suit. Bailey sat on his car fender and shook his head. "Somehow I know this asshole is going to turn out to be a victim."

Bailey didn't get to finish the cigarette before half a dozen undercover cars and marked units arrived all sliding in like a home plate squeeze play, tires smoking and red lights glaring. Snort bailed out of one of the lead cars, "Outstanding Skipper! This asshole just robbed the Chinese restaurant across from the office and pistol whipped Mr. Wang." Snort looked down at the unconscious suspect, "Asshole!"

Bailey emitted a sigh of relief. " No big thing." He wiped his wrist across his forehead and took a drag on his smoke. As an afterthought he jerked the cigarette out of the suspects mouth and handed it to Snort who immediately lit up and smoked it.

CHAPTER 11

Headquarters

Milquetoast had to make a big thing about it. It was after 9:00 PM and the paperwork from the bust was finally under control. Bailey found himself standing in front of the aircraft carrier desk again. As usual Milquetoast's shirt was starched but, disgusting yellow stains in the pits became grossly obvious as he cupped his hands behind his head and leaned back in his chair.

"Amazing. A robbery occurs while you're sitting in my office, you get a call, and you respond from Headquarters and make the pinch. Outstanding work. I almost feel like I was part of this arrest. I almost feel responsible for catching the guy by having you up here."

"I couldn't have done it if you hadn't let me leave, Chief." Bailey would say damned near anything to get out of there.

"Well there's a commendation in it for you, Bailey. I don't really appreciate your management style, but you are one hell of a street cop."

"It was a team deal, Chief. Let's split the difference and give the guys a unit citation." Bailey knew Milquetoast was bullshitting. He had no intention of giving any of them squat.

"Wonderful, wonderful, I'll present it at council and then I'll say a few words. Maybe I'll mention how I was part of this thing by having you up here then letting you go. Certainly, the council will love it." Milquetoast swiveled his chair towards his portrait of President Carter he kept on the office wall behind his desk.

"Thanks Chief, can I go? I have a dental appointment."

"At ten o'clock at night?"

"It's one of those HMO 24 hour deals." Bailey hated lying but somehow worked past it.

"That's fine son, that's fine." Milquetoast's eyes glazed into a trance as he fantasized about the Mayor giving him an award for the apprehension he led on the robber.

***

Bailey ran to the report writing area and got on the phone. He dialed up Denise. "Hey, it's me, Frank. Is the bath water still warm?"

"It's 10 o'clock... Things here are very cold." She slammed the phone down into the cradle hard enough to hurt Bailey's ear.

"Crap!"

Diverting to plan two, Bailey dialed Pizza Hut and ordered a home delivery. If he picked up a six pack on the way he would just have time to beat the driver there and write him a possible bad check for the pie and still have a pleasant evening at home. Tomorrow is another day. Besides, when Denise finds out she dumped on him after he was a big hero for catching the robber, tomorrow night might be.... extraordinary... to say the least. Guilt is great; the ultimate aphrodisiac.

Within 30 minutes Frank settled into 'Rio Bravo' for the fortieth time and wolfed down a two item pizza.

At the end of his second beer the pager buzzed. Bailey fumbled for it and pushed the access button.

"The Chief's office? What is he doing in this late?"

Bailey's first thought was something happened to one of the guys. The Chief hadn't directly paged him in his entire career. He dialed frantically and grabbed a mylanta tablet to settle the sinking feeling in his stomach.

"Chief Milton." Bailey heard him answer curtly.

"This is Frank Bailey, sir."

"Frank, something awful has happened. I need you and at least ten of your men in here immediately." The Chief's voice sounded high pitched with stress.

Frank took a deep breath anticipating the worst, "Was it one of ours, sir?"

"I'm afraid so, Frank. I don't know how to say this... It was the Mayor."

"My God, who would want to kill the Mayor?" Frank felt sincere affection for the old man. He wasn't much of a Mayor since his mind started slipping, but he had always been decent to Frank, and he never played politics with the police department.

"Kill the Mayor? What are you talking about?" the Chief sounded confused.

"Well, what happened to the Mayor? Why did you call me?" Frank was confused and getting annoyed.

"I don't know how to say this Frank, so I'll just come out and tell you straight. Someone defecated on his desk tonight. The janitors found it."

Frank placed his hand over the mouthpiece quickly to conceal the belly laugh. He regained his composure long enough to respond, "No shit?"

Milton didn't get it, "I'm afraid it's true. We have to get to the bottom of this right away. I didn't know who else to assign, sex crimes, burglary...I guess you people at the SIU were the first one to come to mind when I heard about it."

Frank wondered what he meant by that.

The Chief continued, "Needless to say, I want you down here immediately. I have a command center set up at City Hall

"Thanks for the vote of confidence Chief, I'll meet you at his office in thirty or forty minutes." Bailey hit the disconnect button and laid on the floor laughing for five minutes before he initiated his squad call-out.

***

Thursday morning 0100
Graveyard shift

The first page was to Sergeant Hank James. The old sergeant seldom got excited, unless confronted by people telling him how to be sensitive, and tended to keep to himself for the most part. That made him Bailey's kind of guy. The phone rang and Bailey picked it up, relishing the anticipation of telling his old buddy about the call from the Chief. He was picturing James, probably sleeping in his recliner with an empty bottle of Miller's High Life between his legs, looking kind of like Al Bundy.

"Bailey." Frank said.

Hank answered, "Frank, did you page me?"

"Hank... Somebody defecated on the Mayor's desk tonight."

"Defecated?"

"You know, took a dump on it." Bailey rolled his eyes back, thinking about how stupid this sounded.

"No shit?"

"I'm serious as crushed nuts," Bailey didn't sound serious as he desperately fought the urge to laugh.

Hank didn't respond right away. "Well... Are you saying I did it?"

"Hell no, Hank... What makes you say that?"

"Well then why the hell are you calling to tell me?"

"Because we're on the case."

James was now totally confused, "A case of what, Diarrhea?

"Just get your guys and Mickey's guys down to Headquarters. I'll explain down there. And tell those morons to keep their comments to themselves. Somebody thinks this is almost important."

Hank sounded suspicious, "And this ain't some kind of fucking joke right?"

"I wish to fuck it was."

"On my way."

Bailey gargled with Listerine, ate some peanuts to mask his beer breath, then washed those down with a Diet Coke. He grabbed a fresh shirt off the 'fairly clean' pile in the laundry room, pulling it on as he finished the last sip of soda. He was ready to face Milquetoast and the next dirty thankless job on the agenda.

Mayor's Office

City hall was in chaos. Bailey exited the elevator on the eighth floor, encountering the Mayor's receptionist. She sat behind her desk sobbing and pulling tissues out of a box to the tune of about ten per minute. Bailey wasn't sure if it was the beer or he was really hearing a pattern. She sobbed for a few seconds, made three little bugle toots with her nose, then sobbed for a few seconds more.

She stopped her synchronized honking long enough to stare bugged eyed at him for a few seconds then started sobbing again.

Finally, Bailey saw recognition creep in and she spoke. "Oh, Officer Bailey, who would do anything like this? What is this town coming too?" She paused and became indignant in the way only self-important secretaries can. She pointed a finger at Bailey accusingly and shrieked "What are you doing about it?"

Bailey looked her over, then thought to himself that she had probably been a babe in her day. He figured that the Mayor probably thought of her as a young dish. He couldn't help but wonder if the Mayor ever got lucky with the old bat. Bailey experienced the sudden feeling of a reality check when he realized he had been out with worse, far worse. He pinched the bridge of his nose with his index finger and thumb, massaging the area with a calming effect.

He ignored the woman and walked past her into the Mayor's office. He found the room in shambles. The only friendly face was Adolph, the lab guy, who grinned from ear to ear and waved, giddy as a kid at Christmas.

Frank hadn't seen so much brass since the FBI steak fry, the little feed the FBI puts on for all the Fed wanna-be's and suck-ups. Bailey never got invited.

As Bailey gazed around the room, he noticed the Mayor himself, was conspicuously absent.

Bailey noted all the Chiefs, Captains, and lab personnel surrounding what appeared to be a disgusting human turd on the Mayor's desk. He wondered if any of them stuck a finger in it to taste and declare, "Pure shit" like on old TV shows.

Bailey got closer and muttered to himself in amazement, "Christ, they marked around it with white chalk like a friggin body!" Bailey diverted his gaze to keep from laughing. We're too late, it must be dead, he thought to himself. He placed his hand over his eyes to try to conceal that he was on the verge of breaking out into hysterical laughter.

Milquetoast approached him and put his hand on Bailey's shoulder. "It's all right, son. Believe me, I've seen worse."

Bailey had seen worse crime scenes too, but never had he seen the monumental stupidity of government stacked quite so high. He turned and headed for the door when he felt a tug at the upper sleeve of his jacket. He looked over his shoulder, then jumped back, startled as he faced a blurry three-eyed monster. He blinked at the glare, then recognized the face of the Chief Chemist of the crime lab, Adolph Von Hammel. Adolph wore his usual thick horn rim glasses, supplemented with a surgical mask and one of those reflecting metal disks on his head. Bailey recovered from the sight of the six foot six scientist only to wonder why he was wearing all the Dr. Frankenstien get-up. Bailey knew Adolph loved to parade around Headquarters in his lab get-up, but he never saw him wear it outside. Bailey wondered if the weird clothes were something like a cross-dresser fetish or something.

"Adolph, you scared me there for a second." Bailey found out too soon why the lab man wanted him, as Adolph thrust what appeared to be a poopsicle in his face.

"Vaht do you make of this specimen, Frank?" Von Hammel had his arm around Bailey's shoulders forcing their faces closer to the feces specimen on the wooden stick.

"I think you better get that turd out of my face before I puke, you goofy kraut!"

"Ha, you always maken me der laugh, Frank. Always a good joke, ja! But seriously, look at der texture and der foreign substances. If I can tell you vaht is the composition, will it be of help?"

Frank slowly pushed the German's hand away from his face. "Anything you can give me, I'll pass on to my detectives, Adolph." Frank regretted the day he befriended the big, lonely immigrant when the scientist first joined the department to head up the crime lab. Adolph was nothing if not loyal to his first 'Pal' on the PD. Frank recalled that he was probably the only sworn member of the department who befriended Adolph. Most cops, being paranoid anyway, tended to distance themselves from the hulking foreigner.

Adolph wandered away, staring at the specimen, while Frank made for the door. The Chief and Captain Tanner, the Detective Bureau Commander, stopped Bailey again. "Where are you going so soon, Lieutenant?" Tanner asked.

"I have to brief the troops at HQ, Cap." Bailey felt uncomfortable ever giving these two clowns a straight answer, but in this case, the truth couldn't hurt him.

"Well, what's your plan of action? What's our stated operational objective?," Milton inquired trying to pose in a commanding manner.

"As far as I know, we could begin with burglars who have been known to defecate at crime scenes, and persons who have made threats against City Hall. I was going to send Sergeant James' crew on one angle and Sergeant Mickey Delgado's on the other. As far as an operational objective, I guess we're going to try and arrest the suspect." Bailey always hated it when the administrators came back from a management seminar with a bunch of the latest executive catch phrases.

"Well what about the letter, Lieutenant?" said Tanner accusingly. He always left people with the impression that he suspected they were stealing from the company.

"Letter?" Bailey's mind reeled. "Is there a ransom for this turd?" Bailey started wondering if he was having some kind of psychotic hallucination or worse. Was he losing his grip on reality, or had everybody else gone mad?

"The letter that was left beside... that." said Tanner pointing toward the feces with his nose.

"I wasn't informed of any letter." Bailey's jaw set at the angle it takes prior to losing his temper. He always felt that Tanner took steps to conceal things from people, then tried to make them feel foolish by acting as though they've overlooked the obvious. It didn't make Bailey feel foolish, just annoyed. Milton gave Tanner the 'way to keep them on their toes' nod of approval. Tanner handed the letter to Bailey. It was in an evidence bag, but under the current conditions Bailey pulled on some plastic gloves prior to handling it, just to be safe.

He read out loud, "The King must be set free." He shook his head as he looked at the scrawled printing. "What the hell is this supposed to mean?" He asked no one in particular.

"That's what we're counting on you to find out," said Milton. "We have a news blackout on this until we get a substantial lead, so I suggest you get your people on it. I'll look forward to reviewing your reports tomorrow afternoon. Now clean up this mess!"

Bailey did a quick double take from Milton to the feces.

"No, not that mess, I mean solve this thing... And quickly!" He turned his back to the Lieutenant.

Bailey took Milton's rude behavior as a dismissal and quietly headed back toward the door. He was hoping there were some aspirins left in the bottle he kept in the car. He walked out, almost making it to the Mayor's door frame. A fast walking Curtis Gilmore, City Manager, nudged Bailey aside, as he pushing his way through the confusion. Gilmore was a kick-butts and take names kind of guy. He ran the city with an iron fist and crushed anyone who got in his way. Bailey always thought he would be good at organizing stuff like the Tianamen Square Massacre or perhaps being dictator of a banana republic. Shit, the guy was a walking human rights violation.

    At any rate, he totally ignored lowly Lieutenant Bailey and started haranguing the Chief and Captain. Bailey enjoyed the scene for a few seconds then quickly made for the exit before they tried to drag him back into that looney bin.

CHAPTER 12

Undercover cop Billy Cardanza received the group page. He phoned in to the voice mail box the Street Crimes Apprehension Team used for call outs. He started feeling the adrenaline rush he always got when the pager went off with an 'ALL CALL' message. It usually meant an armed robbery surveillance or something else exciting. He let it get the best of him sometimes. The guys called him 'Hot Dog'. Billy didn't care. Anything for a bust, anything for the little shot of adrenaline to pump up with. Besides, if he proved himself he could probably earn a better nickname like the old guys had, The Blade, Taz, Booger or Pappy.

Operating on the limited information he received on the phone, Billy headed from his home to the main station briefing room. The call-out, his sergeant told him, involved a cryptic message, something about a guy in the area of City Hall taking a shit. "Must be some fuckin' pervert," Billy thought out loud. As he drove around the northeast corner of City Hall, his headlights flashed on the shrubbery near the statue of the Parma City founders.

Near City Hall

Gus Stephens, park bum and professional panhandler had trouble digesting the free dinner from the homeless shelter. There was just too much spice in the meat loaf. He had picked up a quart of Night Train wine at the liquor store to soothe his throat. As he guzzled the wine, he toked on one of the three joints a passerby had given him during his stint on a street corner with his cardboard sign. He had knocked off about half the Night Train when it suddenly hit him. He broke out in a sweat and felt the unmistakable stomach curdling knot of a sudden diarrhea attack. He threw down his 'Agent Orange' sign, dove into some bushes by an old statue, dropped his drawers and let it rip.

***

The only thing Cardanza could see was *a bare buttocks that suddenly spewed brown liquid substance all over the marble base of the statue,* or so his report would later read. He jammed his brakes, throwing the car into a panic slide, bailed out with his 9mm Glock in one hand and his badge in the other, and yelled "Freeze!" It was the best challenge that came to mind at the moment, although somehow he felt it sounded inappropriate.

The bum, in a foul mood anyway, pointed his bare ass towards the officer and yelled "Fuck you, pig!" then spewed more diarrhea in the officer's general direction.

Cardanza stumbled as he lurched backwards. Slipping in feces, he almost dropped his badge causing a sympathetic reflex response in his gun hand, and he accidentally squeezed off a shot. The round hit the statue breaking off a chip of marble that ricocheted into the flesh of Gus's bare buttocks. Billy's eyes widened in panic and revolt as blood and copious amounts of diarrhea sprayed from the astonished bum's butt as he scrambled away into the night screaming.

Cardanza grabbed his radio and kicked out a 9-9-8, officer involved shooting, that hit the airwaves as Bailey was briefing his two sergeants on the Mayor's case.

"Shit, that's Billy Cardanza." Sergeant Mickey Delgado blurted, his mouth hanging open after he said it. Hank James and Bailey didn't stick around to look. They sprinted for the door and headed for the crime scene.

***

Billy didn't go into foot pursuit. He was in a state of shock, not exactly sure what happened. He holstered the gun and sat on the fender of his car until help arrived. The first back-up was Snort, a fellow detective from the Street Crimes Squad.

Snort got the story from Billy and made a broadcast to 'attempt to locate a possibly injured person.' Snort was an experienced street animal and he knew when damage control was needed. A broadcast of a wounded indecent exposure suspect with an acute diarrhea problem would have started a media feeding frenzy. Snort stashed the rattled young detective in the back of his car and coordinated a search of the area with the first uniform sergeant at the scene.

Snort made a general announcement to officers crowding in to see what they were doing. Shit, he thought as he pushed back an encroaching group of Blue Suits, these guys are worse than the damned citizens. Nosy bastards. "Why don't you assholes set up the fucking perimeter and quit gawking. I'm trying to debrief this fucking guy!" The old detective mother-henned Billy, protecting him from the inquiries of his curious fellow officers until Bailey and James could arrive.

The nosy officers scrambled away stretching yellow crime scene tape all over the area.

Bailey and James pulled up and stepped out of their car. Bailey looked around at the well lit but foul smelling crime scene with disgust. "What in the world happened here?" He nodded towards Billy sitting in the back of the car, "Is he okay?"

Snort shook his head in the affirmative and lit up a Marlboro he borrowed off a passing motor officer. "Well Boss, as close as I can figure it, Billy was shit at and missed, then the bum was shot at and hit."

Hank James butted in, his old ghetto voice inflection overriding his usual soft spoken style, "What the fuck are you talking about, you ugly mother fucker? When the Lieutenant asks you a question, give him a straight answer god-damn it... We're supposed to be professionals you fat fucking cock-sucker! Is a little courtesy too much to fucking expect?"

"Sorry Sarge," Snort came to a very rough form of attention and rephrased his report, "Billy heard we were going after some pervert who does burglaries and takes a dump at the scene or something and he saw some loser taking a healthy one on the statue over there so he called him out and I guess he tried to blast old Billy."

James frowned, "You mean he pulled a gun?"

"Not exactly Sarge, he let loose with a blast of diarrhea and Billy fell down and the gun went off. The perp took off north through the park and over to the government housing area." Snort looked down at his feet, "I think Billy hit him in the left cheek."

Bailey interrupted, "You mean he popped a cap on this asshole for blasting a load of shit at him?"

Snort shrugged, "I think it was an A.D. Skipper...The guy wouldn't stop walking backward towards him, just shit blasting out of his ass like a fire hose, and I guess it startled Billy, I mean, really, who ever heard of something like that before... Then Billy slipped and the gun went off. He's pretty scared."

The detectives flinched at a piercing scream.

"Yuck!"

They looked over to see an officer dancing around cursing. He apparently arrived late and accidentally stepped in a puddle of diarrhea.

"I'm going to burn these fucking shoes!"

The detectives ignored the interruption and stepped further away from the foul smelling scene.

"Listen", Bailey put his hand on Snort's shoulder and spoke softly, "You don't say anything to anybody unless you clear it with me, understand?"

"You got it, Boss." Snort nodded his head and quickly disappeared into the crowd.

James drew closer to Bailey and apologized in a whisper, "I'm sorry about Snort's fucking mouth, Boss. I'll catch him later and kick his ass for being discourteous. The fucker."

"Chill Hank, Snort didn't mean anything by it. Besides that, he's not a supervisor and a gentleman like us anyway."

James agreed enthusiastically, "That ain't no bullshit!"

Bailey and James got into the front of the car with Detective Billy Cardanza. Billy kept his head down.

Bailey lit up a smoke and gazed out the front windshield. "One... you don't take down a maggot without a backup... That will never happen again."

Billy nodded his head in silent agreement, knowing he'd violated one of the Lieutenant's primary rules.

Hank James pulled a handkerchief out of his pocket and wiped perspiration off his bald forehead as he listened. He almost interjected something but decided to let the Lieutenant handle it.

"Two... If you just saw something suspicious and were taking a quick look to see what it was, prior to calling for a back-up... I still don't like it but... All you saw was something suspicious and you decided to take a quick look... Right?...RIGHT?"

Billy again made a small nodding movement, "Yes sir."

"Three...If someone suddenly charges at you.... And I don't care if they are running forward or backward... If they got pants on or not, it's only human nature to take a step backwards.... And anybody can slip, understand?"

The young detective looked up slowly, " I think so, sir."

Bailey finished, "Fine...and if someone charges at you and throws human bodily fluids at you, no matter how they do it, your life is at some risk... Right?"

The young detective nodded earnestly in agreement, "Yes sir...that's right."

"So look, we won't really know if this loser was shot or not, until we find him again, but some people will treat it like a case of brutality no matter what. You tell the truth. Lying will only jam you up later... But don't make it any worse on yourself." Bailey leaned forward and pulled his wallet out of his back pocket. He thumbed through it until he found a dog eared gray business card. "This guy is a lawyer. He owes me a favor." Bailey handed the card to the detective. "I helped him pour a slab for a new patio at his house a couple of weeks ago. Call him, tell him I told you to call and have him get his ass down to Headquarters right away."

Bailey leaned over the back of the front seat and spoke nose to nose with Billy, "You fucked up. You didn't do anything that couldn't have happened to somebody else, and you damned sure don't deserve to get crucified by some rank-climbing, egg-sucking piece of shit from IA or the press. If you get legal assistance right away they'll back off. They usually only pick on the weak. Snort will help you with your report."

"Thanks, Boss."

"Don't thank me Billy. Just don't ever fuck up like this again. Don't ever tell anybody about this little talk, and for damned sure don't start bragging around the station that you're Dirty Harry or I'll have Sergeant James kill your dumb ass and bury you in the desert.. GOT IT?"

Billy looked at the scarred wrinkled faces of the two surly middle-aged cops. James had a twitch in his jaw line as though he might be in the process of having a brain embolism or something. Billy was pretty sure if he caused any more grief for the unit the old sergeant might really kill him. "Yes, sir... I got it.... Thank you."

"Let's go." Bailey got out of the car and waved over an officer in a marked unit. "Officer, take this detective to an interview room at Criminal Investigations, and don't let anyone talk with him until Snort gets there to stand by with him."

The uniform officer started to comply with the order but suddenly stopped. He looked back to Bailey with a quizzical look on his face, "Who?"

Bailey started to say a name but couldn't remember who Snort really was. He gave James a frustrated look and the sarge fired back at him with the 'you senile old fart' look.

Hank answered for him, "Detective Murphy, big mean biker looking bastard who's uglier than a gunny sack full of hairy armpits." James pulled his hanky out again and wiped more perspiration off his face. Damned Arizona heat. He should have stayed in Detroit.

The rookie street officer was putting his gear in the back seat so Billy could sit up front, "Oh.... Snort... Yes sir!"

The officer and Billy got in the car. Billy gave his supervisors a feeble wave, despondent as a puppy heading for the pound.

As the patrol car pulled out, the City Manager pulled in followed by the Chief and Captain Tanner.

Frank Bailey was getting tired, and his pager was now going off with another call about every fifteen seconds. He didn't need Gilmore and his two butt-boys humping his leg right now.

"Did they get him? Did they get the bastard?" Milton was frantic.

"An officer had a confrontation with a possible lead, Chief. The suspect escaped into the 'hood' and the troops are trying to get him picked up right now." Bailey took a deep breath.

Milton looked pissed off, "Do you mean to tell me he got away?"

Before Bailey could come up with an answer he was interrupted by the City Manager.

"I understand there was gunplay?" Gilmore put his hand on the Chief's shoulder and pushed him out of the way.

Bailey answered professionally. "Yes sir, a shot was fired. Apparently the suspect attacked the officer with some type of bodily fluid, not unlike what happens in the prisons to the correction officers quite frequently. It's all under investigation as we speak." Bailey remained straight faced as he spoke. James turned away towards their undercover car, trying to decide what stream of shit was worse, Bailey's or the diarrhea.

"We'll need a full report in the morning Lieutenant. Complete details." Tanner wasn't good at concepts so he specialized in details.

"Yes sir." Bailey hesitated as the three turned away and walked back to their cars. "Chief..."

"Yes, Lieutenant Bailey? The Chief turned with impatience.

"The officer wasn't hurt... He's fine."

The trio all started making grim faces like they were really concerned. "Good... Glad to hear it. I was wondering when you were going to tell us." The Chief looked at Tanner. "That's a relief... That the officer's okay, isn't it?"

Tanner agreed. "Yes, it is. A relief."

The Chief got in his car.

Bailey didn't quite make it to his car before the lab truck driven by Von Hammel pulled up beside him. "Frank...Is there more fecal specimens here, Ja?"

"Knock yourself out, Adolph..." Bailey started to turn away but he had to ask, "Can you really tell if it's the same guy's... fecal matter?"

"Well, I can't tell you if it is, but I can tell you if it isn't about 40% of der time." Adolph pursed his lips as he concentrated, "If der specimens are adequate."

"Well there's diarrhea shit over about ten square yards there." Bailey guestimated the ground coverage. "If that's not adequate..." Bailey recalled the blood at the OJ case and decided that maybe he was overstepping the boundaries of his scientific knowledge about what was adequate. After that case, it was generally accepted that samples weren't adequate. If you wanted to prove something you needed *all* the suspect's blood at the scene.

"Diarrhea?... Diarrhea?" Adolph looked puzzled.

"You know... Runny grunts, the squirts, liquid fecal matter that stinks real bad ..Adolph.. You know.. Diarrhea!" Bailey's stress levels approached the intolerant range.

"Not good," Adolph shook his head in disapproval.

"Tell me about it. I feel like I have to puke every time I draw a breath over there."

The German chemist spoke as if he were scolding a little kid. "No, No, No....The stool sample from the Mayor's office are very solid... Not likely that the suspect would have so much diarrhea shortly afterward unless it was somehow intentionally done."

Bailey had heard enough about the scientific properties of human excrement for one day, "Call me if you come up with something Adolph. I have to go to Headquarters." He got into the car with Sergeant James.

"Frank", James gazed out the passenger window.

"Yeah".

"I've been thinking. This place is getting too weird. I might put papers in for a transfer to the motor squad again. I kind of miss the old Kawasaki."

"Hank".

"Yeah".

"If I'm stuck here, you're stuck here." The Lieutenant didn't even look at James as he said it. "Besides, if your wife thought I ever let your sorry ass back on one of those murder cycles, she'd kill me right after she cut your nuts off."

"Well I'd miss you and my nuts, but this chasing around after people who are taking these felony dumps is getting too strange. I mean.... Where's the glamour?"

Bailey turned and looked at James like he had a big booger hanging out of his nose. "Since when are you glamorous. You're a fat old bald headed slob like me... except I ain't so fat."

"You know what I mean god-damn it, high speed car chases, big busts, foxy young female rookies lusting for my body."

Bailey threw his cigarette butt out the window in disgust, "That's it... You've been watching TV again, haven't you?"

Hank James' facial expression reminded Bailey of when defense attorney 'Flea' Bailey got caught lying about his so called 'Marine to Marine' interview with the witness at the O.J. trial. Indignant, but guilty as charged.

Bailey figured he better nip this motor cop fantasy in the bud, so he continued hammering James.

"For crying out loud Hank, your kids are older than most of these rookies and you don't drive over forty on the freeway." Bailey quit nagging when he saw his old friend hang his head. The Lieutenant calmed down, "If you quit your whining, you old fart, maybe next week I'll take you to the Jaguar Club for an administrative liquor inspection. That usually cheers you up."

In spite of what he said, Bailey couldn't help but wonder if Hank was right. Maybe things were getting just a little too weird.

They rode to the station in silence.

In a dumpster
In the 'hood'

Gus Stephens sat concealed in the safety of his favorite trash dumpster. He found an old pillowcase inside and fashioned a bandage for the slight wound on his buttocks. He decided then and there he would hole up until daybreak, then he was heading for Las Vegas. The Arizona cops were just too weird. This whole town was too weird.

CHAPTER 13

In his modest home in the central part of the city, the elderly Mayor was dreaming of the curvaceous Vanna White. He asked for a vowel and Vanna was trying to tell him something but the damned ringing drowned her out. Groggily he shook his head as he awakened enough to reach for the telephone. "Who the hell is this?" The Mayor suddenly felt refreshingly clear headed.

"Your Honor, it's City Manager Gilmore. I need to report some important information and time is of the essence."

An irritated Mayor grew concerned, " It's not one of our firemen or policemen is it?"

"No, no, no.... This is serious. Someone...an unknown perpetrator, has defecated on your desk."

"I'm sorry?" Inquired the Mayor, unsure if he heard correctly.

"You know... defecated... on your desk."

"I know what 'defecated' is Gilmore... Why the hell are you calling me? You know at my age I have enough trouble sleeping at night without you calling me about every little thing. Will the janitors clean it up?"

"Well actually sir, I had the desk taken to the crime lab for processing. With the uh... feces."

"Crime lab?" the Mayor shook himself awake. "Somebody poops on a piece of furniture and you have the crime lab out? Just have the janitor clean it up and go back to bed." The Mayor began to get angry, "What time is it anyhow?"

"It's three o'clock sir."

"When did this heinous crime occur?" The Mayor looked over but couldn't make out the face of his clock without his trifocals.

"We found it about quarter till ten, sir." Gilmore was nervous. He guessed the Mayor's next question, " I didn't want to call you until I knew something."

"That will be a cold day in Hell. Well, since you have awakened me with this big news alert in the middle of the night, I'm not coming in tomorrow. I'm going to the doctor and then I'm going over to the senior center. Goodnight Gilmore.' the Mayor slammed the phone.

He got up to get a glass of milk. He was irritated but as he approached the refrigerator he couldn't remember why. It seemed like the phone had been ringing.

He poured his milk into a small clear glass. He noticed a sticky-note on the counter, 'Senior Center, Thursday morning'. He smiled as he wondered who the note was for. He went to his closet and pulled his suit on over his pajamas and went back to bed.

As he rolled over to go to sleep he laughed at his special little joke. Nobody messes with Vanna. Not as long as Mayor... Mayor... Oh well, what ever the name was.

CHAPTER 14

Thursday morning - 0700 hrs.

Detective Denise Downey came in two hours early to prepare for her staff presentation. She sorted through the pile of reports on her desk. She had three confirmed molestations of small boys in the city during the past year. For a city of over 300,000 that figure was low on the nationwide average, but for Downey, even one case was unacceptable. Downey also considered that only a small number of the cases that occurred were probably ever reported, if three were reported, she probably had ten or twenty she didn't know about.

The victims ranged in age from five to nine. None of them were of similar appearance. Two were white and one was Hispanic. All were dropped off in an alley after being traumatized by the suspect. None of the boys could give a decent description. In all of the cases, the child was lured from a front yard or play area. The only real lead was the black electrical tape used to tie the victims.

Denise felt her eyelids getting heavy as she strained over the handwritten reports. God, if I could only get a good nights sleep, she thought. But it was the dreams. The dreams of abuse at the hands of a molester, the abuse of a brutal first husband, and now the self-abuse of trying to help these poor victims, and in turn, cleanse her past. But the more she worked these child-victim cases, the more she dwelled on the past.

She pushed the papers away and leaned back in her chair. Denise thought of Frank. She had been seeing him quietly for the past year. Her friends told her to stay away from him, he was older and since that old guy killed himself, Bailey seemed to be more moody and cynical than usual. One of her friends called him a head case.

Well, maybe she would rethink the whole relationship, if that's what is was, after he stood her up last night.

She felt there was some potential with Frank but if he didn't show some interest in a more permanent relationship soon, she was going to have to move on. Frank was a gentle man, at least with her. She massaged her temples, "Oh please let this work out," she whispered to herself, deciding to forgive him for his faux pas the night before, after giving him a severe chewing out.

She grabbed a stack of computer data that came in from Records. She thumbed through the pile looking for mention of child pornography or sex offenders.

She popped out her contacts and put on her glasses. She had trouble reading the tiny print without something and the dust storms in the greater Phoenix area were wreaking havoc on her eyesight.

She found a spread sheet on convicted sex offenders from within Arizona and browsed through the names. She noticed most of them didn't get any serious jail time. She ran her finger down the time served column. "Damn, this one only got three days in jail and mandatory counseling," she whispered. She looked at his sheet. Computer programmer.

Nickname, Dingo, the same moniker that continued to show up on the Internet kiddy porn chat lines.

She read further down the columns. He's last listed in Flagstaff over two years ago, then nothing. So much for probation. I wonder if this could be the same guy?

Denise picked up the phone and called the records section. "Hello Jenny, this is Detective Downey, can you run a utilities address check for the past two years on this name, James Davis Coker, aka Dingo? Thanks..."

Downey waited a minute or so before the clerk came back on the line. "Okay, thanks. Yeah, I'll be down to pick it up."

Downey pulled her gun out of the desk drawer and holstered it for the walk downstairs to records. A lot of detectives just locked their weapon up in their desks when they were working in the building, but Downey saw too many of them get paged and head out to the street, forgetting to pick up their gun first. Downey had no patience for the tactically retarded.

She hustled down the stairwell, personal policy to avoid using the elevator, and hustled around the corner into the records section. Downey found the information she ordered on the counter tagged with a yellow sticker with her name scratched on it.

Denise made eye contact with the clerk who helped her and mouthed a thank you. The clerk was busy working on another request and only nodded and smiled.

Denise scanned the information. A man by the same name moved to the city and opened a utility account about eighteen months ago. Damn.

Council Chambers

That morning the City Council held an emergency meeting. Gilmore sat at the table head with Slim Archwald, the developer turned politician who acted as Mayor whenever the old man wasn't available. He slammed a gavel against a folding table top and called the meeting to order. Slim looked cautiously towards Gilmore like a little kid looking at his teacher during his first piano recital. Gilmore gave an approving parental-like nod.

In the hallway, Chief of Police Milton sat cooling his heels waiting to answer questions if needed. He fretted over his notes, stood up, sat down, and fretted again over the report Bailey spent the night typing up.

The Chief dreaded these affairs. He hated the city council. The arrogant bastards, he thought to himself, these two-bit politicians are always treating me like a lowly servant.

He knew that when he retired and ran for council he wouldn't treat important people, like himself, that way.

In the small special session meeting room the council members looked at each other accusingly. In the Post-Nixon political age, the best way to get ahead was to collect some dirt on another politician or public figure, and pile it on deep and fast in the name of whatever the current rage is; missing children, family values, or law and order for example. This was an especially difficult skill to develop because you had to pile it on someone else before they found out what kind of sleaze-ball you were and started piling some themselves. Slim Archwald, known as Captain Corruption among most of the local police officers, was a master sleaze-ball. He was often suspected of using his position for inside information, special breaks from building inspectors, and bid fixing to benefit his construction and development companies. He got the nickname 'Slim' do to his gaunt appearance, caused by a near obsession with running.

He was frequently seen jogging the streets of his upscale north east city neighborhood. He had a weasel face decorated with a mustache not unlike those sported by villains in the silent movies. He enjoyed wearing construction type clothing to meetings, so he would appear to be a little on the blue collar side. Although his usual attire was polyester suits when he was away from the prying eyes of City Hall, he felt compelled to maintain the image of a man of the people.

Slim hated the cops and the cops hated him. He understood why they needed a few people around the police department to keep a lid on the minority populations, but all in all they were a waste of money. He championed the idea, and would bend the ear of whoever would listen, as to how it would be cheaper to privatize the police as much as possible with a few minimum wage security guards. Today, however was a different story, "Mr. Gilmore, do you suspect political terrorism is involved in this attack and should I... we... expect further attacks or any escalation of the violence?"

As the other five council members looked on with concern, Gilmore responded, "The Mayor has directed me to take command of this situation. He was so distraught with the outrage that he was weakened and unable to attend this meeting today. As a matter of fact I recommended that he see his doctor and I believe he is following my advice as we speak. The first order of business is to keep a lid on this and prevent a circus with the local papers and those fascist talk radio bastards. I want a total media blackout initiated to minimize my... our risks of becoming victims. I don't have any details on additional threats but I have the Chief available to brief us as to what action he recommends.

A council aide went into the hallway and summoned the Chief, who was feverishly reading the notes Bailey had prepared. The Chief stood, straightened his tie and followed the aide into the room. "Good morning ladies and gentlemen." He tried to sound pretentious and failed.

"No time for small talk Milton. Do you have the person or persons in custody at this time, or are we all still at risk here?" Gilmore talked down to the Chief as though Milton was some pervert he just caught window peeping.

Milton felt the rebuke and lost his train of thought. Embarrassed at so obviously having had the air let out of his sails, he replied defensively, "There was an armed confrontation with a possible lead last night."

Slim Archwald gasped, "Then they have escalated to violence!"

Milton was way outside of the paranoia loop of the council, "Excuse me... Who is *they*... and what did *they* escalate?"

Councilwoman Claire DeVincent-Milo, car dealer and left-wing political tigress detected weakness and jumped on the confused Chief with both spike heeled feet, "Don't try and downplay this Chief. You know damned well what we're talking about! TERRORISM!". She was shrieking, "Terrorists are out to get us all!" She slammed her diamond speckled fist on the table.

The Chief was completely lost, "What terrorists, I didn't say anything about terrorists?"

It was Gilmore's turn again. Red-faced, he too was shrieking "Damn it Chief, if they attack government buildings and engage the police in armed confrontation, what else would you call it?" He shook his index finger in the Chief's face as he spoke, intimidating the confused Chief even more. "AND BY GOD, I WANT SOME ACTION!"

Suddenly he stopped and regained his composure. "Chief Milton, I'm sorry. So far they have only gone after the

Mayor. There is no indication that the terrorists are interested in the rest of us at this point."

The Chief sat in his chair in a daze. He couldn't help but wonder, have all these people lost their minds? He knew when he got the turn to be a council person, he would definitely not engage in such rude and erratic behavior. At least not to someone like himself.

Archwald sounded off again breaking the Chief's reverie, "I suggest we act on Mr. Gilmore's recommendation of a news blackout until the Chief," he paused and glared disdainfully at the bewildered lawman, "Can get us some concrete information regarding this case. Until then I believe we should adjourn for forty-eight hours." Archwald slammed a gavel and they all rose from their seats and left the room, leaving Milton sitting alone in council chambers wondering why he hadn't joined the fire department. This never happened to the Fire Chief!

CHAPTER 15

Police Headquarters
Sex Crimes Unit

Downey's desk phone rang once before she picked it up. "Sex Crimes, Detective Downey, may I help you?"

The Chief's secretary identified herself, "Detective, the staff meeting is postponed until tomorrow at 10:00. The copies of your proposal have been distributed to staff and they will be prepared to discuss it then."

Downey didn't let her voice reveal her disappointment. "Thanks ma'am. I'll be there." She hung the phone up and walked downstairs to the break room. Time to chill out, she thought. She wondered what came up that was so important the staff canceled its standard Thursday morning briefing.

Downey found her sergeant sitting on a plastic chair by the vending machines sipping from a container of chocolate milk.

He saw her come in and spoke first, "Did you get the word?"

"Yeah, tomorrow is another day."

"Yeah, sorry Denise. That's the way it goes around here."

"I know, not your fault Boss."

He straightened in his chair. "Did you hear about the SIU guys catching the armed robber yesterday?"

Her thoughts turned to concern for Frank. "No, what happened?"

"The Chinese market got robbed. Bailey bagged one suspect in the parking garage, the other guys grabbed the accomplice down the street. Big old foot chase. Pretty cool."

Denise tried to appear somewhat disinterested, "Did anyone get hurt?"

"Bailey gave a suspect a shiner is all."

"Neat deal."

"Yeah. The SIU people get all the fun."

Downey was mentally kicking herself for not letting Frank explain the night before.

"Sarge, I have some 'comp' time on the books, would you care if I took the rest of the day off. I got..." she lowered her voice to a whisper, "Female problems."

The old sergeant didn't even like to think about the ramifications of 'female problems'. "Sure, no problem. See you tomorrow."

Denise left to initiate damage control.

***

While the Chief was hunkered at council chambers in shell shock, Emma saw her boss coming down the hallway of the SIU offices. She thought to herself that Bailey looked like an unmade bed. His hair looked like he combed it with a firecracker. The thin, blonde mop was raked straight back clearly revealing his receding hairline. That style usually indicated he was not depressed, but feeling self-confident to the level of dealing with male pattern baldness today. She continued her amateur psycho-analysis by a conducting a review and evaluation of his clothes. His red Hawaiian shirt, wrinkled cotton pants, and scuffed up topsiders usually meant he was having a good day, he was wearing his favorite stuff. She pursed her lips and thought to herself that all that man needs is a good woman to kind of....iron him, or something. Too bad I'm not interested in any more burned-out losers or I might take a stab at the scrawny old fart myself. Maybe put some weight on him.

Emma was in the process of lighting a cigarette but put it out as a gesture of respect just to show the boss she was a loyal trooper. She started to return the smoke to her purse but as he got closer, she could see he already had one in his mouth so she lit up. "Sorry dear, but you look like shit."

"Bad choice of words, Emma." Bailey stopped and took a deep breath, "Buy me a coffee and I'll tell you all about looking like shit, looking at shit, and being in shit...In that order."

"Lucky you, I just hit the ugly teller for twenty bucks. How does breakfast sound?"

Bailey nodded in agreement and mumbled something about how it sounded pretty good. He wondered why nobody he ever got personally involved with, ever treated him this good. Poor Emma, den mother to the demented, paranoid and depressed SIU cops. He looked her over, and decided it would be unfair to the world to have the Mother Theresa of law enforcement taken out of circulation, so he wouldn't make a move on her. Besides, she would probably slap him silly if he tried it.

Emma drove them to Johnson's Best in the West Restaurant with the fake building front. The good looking imitation cowgirl waitresses with tight jeans and fake six shooters strapped on seemed to add a touch of local color to the joint, after all, it was Arizona. The gunbelts and tight wrangler jeans gave birth to the unofficial name for the place used by the cops, Guns and Buns.

Emma ordered toast and coffee while Bailey decided to pig out on a double order of spicy biscuits and gravy.

He shoveled gravy down like he hadn't eaten for a week, working halfway across his plate before he took a breath, "Emma... Do you think I'm getting cynical and paranoid or is the whole world turning to shit?"

"Yes and yes, dear. Don't eat so fast, you'll upset your ulcer. At your age, you can't be too careful."

"Bitch."

"I love you, too."

Bailey pointed his fork at her, "I'm serious Emma, I think, no, I know Milton and Tanner are out to get me. In fact, I'm pretty sure this case has to be some kind of a set-up or something, like in Mission Impossible... This shit can't be real."

"I thought you said Von Hammel told you it was real shit!"

Bailey took a huge slug of coffee then lifted his cup up towards one of the waitresses for a refill, "You know what I mean. None of the Lieutenants in Phoenix, Tempe or even Chandler have to deal with people this fucking goofy. Well, except for that roller-skating activist guy in Phoenix, or maybe that moron who heads that civil rights group. You know, the guy who can't get a real job but tells everybody else how to do theirs. Shit, our lunatics are elected and appointed officials. I mean...what the hell happened to this city?"

Emma set her lipstick-stained cup down on the table, "It means... Sigmond Froid, that Parma City got last pick of the assholes.

She leaned across the table, "Don't make shit so complicated. It ain't your job to save the world from itself. Do your twenty and get the hell out. Give those scumbags what they want, then sit back and wait for the eagle to shit every other Thursday. Now, let's get out of here before you get any weirder."

CHAPTER 16

Claire DeVincent-Milo left the council meeting in her red BMW and drove at warp factor nine to her car dealership. She slid sideways to a screeching halt in the parking lot and ran up the stairs as fast as her spiked heels and black leather miniskirt would allow her. She slammed the door and threw her notebook on the desk.

Claire, looking fairly attractive compliments of her facelift, breast enhancements and butt tucks, stared at her oil painting of the copper domed Arizona State House on the wall. "I want to be governor! I want to be governor, I want it, I want it, I want it!"

She had decorated her office as an exact replica of the 9th floor executive suite of the Governor of Arizona. Claire was bored with her car dealership and her thirty-five year odyssey of collecting husbands, divorce settlements and alimony that had made her one of the richest women in Arizona. She developed an interest in politics and found that the sense of power that went with political clout was a bigger turn on than a Burt Reynold's Cosmo layout.

Claire's imagination followed a loose stream of conscious thought. There had already been a woman governor and a car dealer governor, but never a woman car dealer governor who looked so damned HOT! She ran her hand along one of her liposuctioned hips.

Claire was shrewd and ruthless. She knew opportunity when she saw it and it didn't take her long to realize that the Mayor had a political gold mine dumped on his desk in the form of a smelly fecal specimen. When this story hit the papers, TERRORIST STALKS MAYOR, it would be the chance of a lifetime to bravely stand in front of TV cameras and denounce terrorism and violence. Too bad it was wasted on that senile old fart who's thrill of the day was to wander aimlessly through the central part of the city looking for where he parked his car. No ambition, no goals, no purpose. She scowled as she thought about it. Everybody in town loved the old Mayor. He didn't need a political windfall to get re-elected... If the old fool decided to get re-elected.

Claire knew that to be Governor, she had to be Mayor. If the old coot didn't run then she had a shot. She sat in her leather executive chair and pouted. Why couldn't the terrorist have pooped on her desk? She wanted the attention. Hell, she needed the attention. Life was so unfair.

***

Archwald jumped into his '71 Chevy Malibu four-door and drove directly to his small office at his construction company headquarters. He paced back and forth across the cheap indoor-outdoor carpeting that covered the eight by ten floor of the CEO office. All he could think about was the lucky break the Mayor fell into. If only the terrorists had targeted him. He knew what to do with a big chance like that. With all the potential TV coverage, his name recognition would bolt him into the Senate seat vacated by McCain's promotion to Secretary of State. Senator Archwald.... It sounded so good just to think it that Slim had to light up a cigarette and relax.

    Somehow he knew he would come up with something and steal the glory from that old fool in the Mayor's office.

***

CHAPTER 17

Bailey dragged his jacket as he slumped along towards the door to his apartment. His tired hands dropped his keys once, picked them up, then successfully manipulated the lock. He was deep in thought, trying to develop rude remarks for whoever the jerks were that would inevitably wake him up, calling with stupid questions all morning. As he wandered in the living room he suddenly realized someone was in his apartment. He started to reach for his gun, but suddenly detected the aroma of coffee, frying bacon, and the unmistakable scent of Denise Downey's expensive Liz Claiborne perfume. He left the state of exhaustion and suddenly disembarked in the town of rejuvenation.

A figure slinked around the edge of the kitchen door. Denise struck a seductive pose as she slowly massaged her thigh with one hand pushing the tail of one of his white dress shirts high enough to reveal there was nothing underneath. Her hair was down and she was wearing the cheap red lipstick that pushed all of Bailey's hormone buttons with the deftness of an elevator operator in the Empire State Building. With her other hand she pulled a little home-made sign out from around the corner with a personal message, WILL PUT OUT FOR FORGIVENESS.

He dropped his jacket and stood slack jawed in awe.

Denise smiled her crooked little smile flashing all those white teeth and whispered in a southern accent that should have been patented by the State of Texas and sold for a million bucks, "Aren't you going to say anything?"

Bailey began to unbutton his shirt, "Yeah. Take the bacon off the stove. We'll eat later."

Denise touched a button on the stove and walked across the room. She put a hand on Frank's chest, "I'll do that for you." She gently pushed his hand away and began to undo the buttons for him.

He wrapped his arms around her pushing the white shirt off her shoulders. He kissed her neck, and moved his hands down her back.

Denise relaxed at his touch until she felt the roughness of his face brush against her breasts. She stiffened, then reached down and grabbed Bailey's shirt, ripping it open, sending buttons flying across the room.

Bailey lifted her in his arms and carried her to the bedroom.

***

Bailey rolled over and reached for his cigarettes on the headboard. He lit one and took a long drag.

Denise stretched then curled up against him.

"Frank, you ever think about doing something else?"

"Honey, we just did everything I ever heard of."

She gently smacked him on the forehead with the palm of her hand. "I mean the job, Frank. God, you have a one track mind."

Bailey turned on his side and faced her, stroking her hair, "Every cop thinks about getting out. What makes you bring that up now?"

"I don't know, it's just, when we're together, here, like this..." She ran her hand over his chest.

Frank smiled, "You've been a cop for ten years Denise, it's normal to hope there really is life after police work."

"No, it's more than that. I used to be proud to be a cop, now I'm starting to think that I don't like what I'm becoming."

"Becoming what?"

"Don't take this wrong Frank... I mean I'm becoming more like you."

He propped himself up on one elbow. "How am I supposed to take a comment like that?"

"I mean, I think the world is a toilet, and everybody in it is a scumbag." She paused. "I'm sorry Frank, this is a hell of a time to get introspective. I just wish there was more than this sense of siege, this feeling that everybody is against us. Sometimes I think there isn't any justice and there isn't going to be any."

"Denise, the world really is a toilet, and there really ain't no justice. I'll alert the media. What's your point?"

"I just wish we could be different, like real people. Hell, Frank, we don't even know any real people. Just maggots and victims... And you and I, we aren't even allowed to know each other, let alone be lovers. Christ, if the Chief ever found out we were together, we would both probably get fired. They all hate you anyway."

He flopped over on his back. "That sure cheers me up." He stared at the ceiling.

"You know what I mean, you're not like those guys. You aren't trying to win the little promotion game and you don't get off on being in charge of people, you just do your job."

"Denise, baby, I love the job. I just hate the sons of bitches who own the company. If the public ever knew what pieces of shit they all are, they'd revolt like the French Revolution, guillotine and all. Shit, I'm so used to being miserable, I think I'm actually starting to like it."

She flopped on her back and stared at the ceiling too. "Frank, tell me there is going to be something someday worth living for. Tell me there is something for us out there."

"Like what, I'll make up something if it will make you feel any better."

"Like you will retire and we can travel the world, or maybe at least leave the city limits and never carry badges again."

"Honey, don't ever, ever tell anybody this, but I wish I could retire. I wish we could go find something. But, I've been out of the real world so long, that I forgot what it's like. I don't think I know how to be happy."

"I could help you learn Frank. Think about it." She kissed him softly. "Think about it." She kissed him again, slowly rolling over on top of him. Straddling him; she kissed his chest softly then took sensuous bites into his shoulder as she manipulated him inside her.

"Think about it."

She gasped as he moved with her thrusting, pushing with her motion. She felt his body tense as he wrapped her in his arms and rolled her over, taking her on his terms. They kissed deeply, as the lovemaking became rougher, more desperate. She felt him lurch forward and knew they were ready. She bit him hard on the pectoral, releasing her own hot burning spot in her belly to explode through her body with her lover's release.

They collapsed together in exhaustion and fell into a deep sleep in each others arms.

5:15 AM

Bailey shot straight up from a sound sleep at the sound of the scream. He instinctively reached for the grip of his .45 and pulled it from between the mattress and box springs.

He started to get out of bed, when he realized Denise was having another dream, a nightmare.

Not knowing what else to do, he softly touched her shoulder and whispered her name, "Denise, honey... Denise."

As he talked he carefully reached over her head and lifted her pistol off the bookcase headboard, securing it out of her reach on his side of the bed. God knows what she's going to do this time, he thought.

She moaned ,"No... No... Get away... Momma...MOMMA!"

Suddenly she started to waken at the sound of Frank's voice.

"Baby, wake up... Please it's okay..." Frank touched her shoulder more firmly, but jerked his hand back at the feel of her skin, icy cold... soaking wet.

She sat up and blinked, slowly realizing where she was. "Oh no, I did it again, didn't I?" She started crying, "Frank, I'm so sorry. God, I can't help it."

He started to hold her in his arms, but she quickly jerked away, then relaxed and settled into the warmth of his hug.

"It's okay, Denise, You can't help it. The man who hurt you died a long time ago. You're safe now, with me."

"I know Frank... I just... I don't know. I guess if I could have dealt with him, confronted him, but back then they covered those things up. My God, he just died of old age, nothing ever happened to him."

Her frightful dream began turning back into conscious frustration and anger.

"Things weren't so bad until this serial molester case developed and all the chat room filth on the net. I know this Dingo connection is something but I can't get anybody interested in helping. God, it's so..." She quit and her eyes began to tear. "Frank, I'm making it worse, aren't I?'"

Frank didn't say anything. He knew about her demons, and he knew only she could save herself from them. He gently kissed her and got up to make coffee.

***

CHAPTER 18

On the Streets

Snort sat in his Buick Grand National listening to the engine idle. God, what a machine, he thought as he remembered back to the day he seized it from a meth dealer in Phoenix. He loved being in the car so much he didn't mind waiting for his chronically late partner Jimmy Bob Rawlins.

Jimmy Bob was a stereotypical hick with nerd tendencies, an unusual breed of individual who seldom appears in nature, except in areas of high mutation such as nuclear waste dumps and law enforcement. Yes, Jimmy Bob was a mutant. Known in law enforcement circles as Rowdy, his interests ranged from hog farming, Hank Williams, and muscle cars to computers, physics, and the space program. Unfortunately for Jimmy Bob 'Rowdy' Rawlins, when he talked about the latter, he still sounded like he was discussing the former. His appearance would leave one to believe that he was preparing for a Ross Perot look-alike contest. At five foot six with a burr haircut, he was a glaring contrast to his big hairy partner Snort.

Snort liked working with Rowdy because he understood Snort's fear of militias, the New World Order, UFOs and Democrats. Rowdy always had scientific explanations for these phenomena, usually based on CIA cover-ups. Snort took comfort in knowing at least one other person in the world knew everybody was out to get them.

Rowdy came out of his house carrying his war bag full of equipment, looked up and down the street, and jogged over to the Grand National. He jumped in without saying anything. Snort put out his cigarette and they headed for the 'Friendly Folks Tavern'. It was a simple infiltration job to penetrate an auto theft gang the intelligence unit suspected was working out of there. They stopped at the impound yard on their way to pick up the old tow truck they seized last year.

They transferred their equipment into the truck and drove in silence for about ten minutes working their way through moderate city traffic.

Snort spoke first, "Rowdy, did you hear about last night, dude?"

Rowdy pushed his horn rim glasses back up his nose with his middle finger. Keeping his eyes focused straight ahead he simply replied, "No." Rowdy avoided being verbose in the event internal affairs had bugged their truck.

Snort looked over at him and wished Rowdy would take the dorky looking Band-Aid off the bridge of his specs. "Some asshole took a shit on the Mayor's desk."

Rowdy was impressed with the news. He wrinkled his nose twice and pushed his glasses back again. "They're not trying to say I did it are they?" Paranoia may be a disease in law enforcement, but it's an epidemic among undercover cops.

"Hell no, man. It was supposed to be blacked out from the media, but I heard on a talk radio show this morning that it was some kind of terrorist thing. Maybe tied into that smoking ban."

Both of them sat in silence, knowingly nodding their heads as they considered the implications. Rowdy spoke up, "I know I didn't do it because I would have taken a dump on Archwald's desk, not the Mayor. The Mayor is the only one of those assholes worth a shit."

The pun escaped them both as they again nodded in silence.

"That ain't all, dude. Billy shot one of them in the ass. He was disguised as a park bum I think, but a caller on the radio show said they had information that it could have been an Iranian. The son-of-a-bitch escaped."

Rowdy looked over at his partner with grim determination as his partner filled him in on the gory details of wounded terrorists, political turmoil, and poor hygiene. He reached into his war bag and pulled out a flash-bang, gas grenade and four extra magazines for their pistols. He divvied the gear between himself and Snort as they stuffed it all in their pockets. Let the Commie hoards come. They wouldn't get Parma City without a fight.

***

Larry Steinburn hated his job, hated his employer, and hated the world. If he could only get enough of a stake to start cooking up some meth, he would be rich instead of leading the shitty life of a lot boy working in that old bitch's car dealership. The manager had been on his ass trying to tie him into the car thefts off the lot and making him go in for a stupid drug screen.

He sat in the 'Friendly Folks Tavern', sucking on a Coors Light for breakfast. He didn't have to be at work until eleven and was hoping to score some crystal, so he could get loaded before reporting for the suck ass job he hated.

He looked up as the two grubby tow truck drivers that had been hanging around lately walked in and sat down at a table near him. One looked like the typical biker type that frequented the joint, and the other looked like that little political guy with the flip charts. He heard them place an order and decided that the little one even sounded like the guy on TV. Too bad he didn't look like the President. That guy gets high and has his way with all the women. Something about a president that does dope is too cool.

Larry noticed what looked like the shape of a crack pipe in the little guy's T-shirt pocket and the M and the 13 on the big guy's denim jacket. He knew they weren't cops because no cop would be as dorky looking as the little guy was. They had to be a couple of loser wildcat tow truckers. Larry decided to hit them up to score some crank. He sauntered up to the table holding his empty beer loosely by the neck. He turned on his charm and used his usual clever intro line. "Hey, what's happening dudes?"

Snort didn't look up, "Blow me, asshole."

"Hey man," Larry was shaking, "No need to get red about it, I was just going to ask about - uh, you know, - a job or something."

"Well, do you see a help wanted sign hanging around my neck, shit for brains? If I had some work, I wouldn't be sitting in this dump talking to you."

Larry stammered something unintelligible and started back for his chair. Snort stopped him. "Wait a minute dude. I didn't mean to be an asshole. Sit the fuck down."

Larry was too scared not to.

Snort started, "Look I don't like to come off like a prick, but this town is crawlin' with fucking narcs, you know what I mean?"

Larry was glad to be in agreement with the surly biker, and like most morons, started talking too much. "No shit, I got busted for a teener of meth by some fucking narc, man. And now my boss at the car lot is trying to make me pee in a bottle, man."

Snort grabbed Larry by the sleeve, "Hey asshole, I thought you said you needed a job. Maybe you are a fuckin' narc."

"No way man, I just want to quit that other job at the car lot before I flunk my pee test. Then I will need a job."

Opportunity was knocking at the door of the partners, but only Rowdy was home, "Did you say, car lot?" He twanged with his Texas hillbilly accent.

"Yeah, you know that old bitch on TV, the one with more facelifts than Captain fucking Kirk?"

Snort still wasn't tuned in, "My TV doesn't work."

Rowdy knew, "Hell yes. That big dealership on west Main."

"Well that bitch, and my asshole manager, think I got something to do with cars and shit getting stolen off the lot and they're making me take a piss test. Assholes."

Snort finally heard the knock and let opportunity walk in, "Well, did you steal the cars?"

Larry actually looked hurt that they thought he was stealing cars, "No way man, one of the other guys I work with is setting up the car thefts, all I ever steal is parts. I'm not an asshole."

Rowdy and Snort shook their heads in agreement at the injustice of it all. Rowdy picked the conversation back up and pointed it where he wanted to go. "We get the same thing.

Some asshole in Phoenix is always trying to get us to steal some cars so he can ship them to Mexico. Says he'll pay top dollar but we ain't got an insider to help us get the son-of-a-bitches. So guys like us eat shit and get blamed for everything while some other asshole gets the big money."

Larry agreed and whined for another half an hour about how unfair life was. Rowdy and Snort listened to the whining as long as they could stand it. They told Larry to keep them in mind if he ever heard of anything they might turn some money on. He gave them his work phone number to call him if they were able to score some crank.

As the two undercover cops walked outside to their truck, Rowdy Rawlins asked Snort the rhetorical question often discussed in police circles, "Can you believe we get paid to do this shit?"

Snort looked down at his buddy and became somewhat philosophical himself, "Sometimes I do feel guilty getting paid to outwit these morons." He shrugged, " Oh well, fuck 'em in the heart."

"Let's get some breakfast."
"Cool."

CHAPTER 19

Bailey's apartment

Bailey got out of a steaming shower, wrapped a towel around his waist, and flopped down on the bed soaking wet. He called out loud for Denise but she was gone. He was sad she didn't take the time to say goodbye. He got up and walked into the kitchen for another cup of coffee and found a note on the kitchen table:

Good morning sunshine,
I had to go into headquarters for my task force presentation. Wish me luck.
I'll see you tonight if you want. Page me.
           Denise

His eyes focused on the red lipstick kiss on the bottom of the note. He found himself wishing she was back in his bed.

The forty-two year old body dragged itself into the bathroom and toweled off. Bailey dressed in a sport coat and slacks, anticipating getting called into the Chief's office again over the shitting and shooting from the night before. His pager was beeping somewhere and he found it and his pants from last night thrown over the dresser mirror. He pulled his underwear off the ceiling fan blade and tossed them in the dirty clothes pile in the corner.

He grabbed a pencil off the dresser and picked up an envelope out of the waste basket.

"The vicious cycle never ends." He wrote down the numbers from the seven pending beeper pages and started making the phone calls from his kitchen phone.

***

Denise tried to keep busy before the staff meeting to avoid a case of the nerves. She worked at the computer station in the sex crimes unit and followed up on the on-line child molester's activity.

She clicked the mouse and switched to the Internet access. She went straight to the web page for chicken hawks, perverts who like young boys. She reviewed a few chat lines frequently used by child molesters. Denise scanned the material mainly looking for local post office boxes and telephones. The detective didn't see anything new and started to close the program when she saw the name on the chat room entry. Dingo.

The missing molester. It had to be the same guy.

Garver called to her that it was time to go, and she signed off.

DeVincent-Milo Car Lot

Larry was greeted by the surly lot manager standing with his hands on his hips and a scowl on his face when he arrived at work at 11:15. "Mrs. DeVincent-Milo wants to see you in her office Steinburn." The manager shook his head, "I hope she's finally going to fire your dumb ass and save me the trouble of doing it."

Larry slinked into the office building, his knees shaking. His thoughts were bouncing off the walls of his burned out skull. He knew he couldn't pass a urine test even if he studied. He thought about making a run for it instead of facing the evil bitch. Larry looked over his shoulder and saw the manager following him. Shit.

He knocked on the door of DeVincent-Milo's office. After a command to enter came from the other side, he slowly pushed it open. Larry expected to see some pentagrams and ram heads inside, but the only thing he noticed was the morning paper laying on her desk.

Claire sat on the edge of her desk showing a lot of leg under the short skirt. She looked up at Larry with a stare that made his knees start shaking worse that before. "Sit down, asshole."

Larry took a chair in front of the desk. The old bitch didn't say anything. She pointed a T.V. remote control at the set in the wall unit behind her desk. A black and white surveillance tape clearly showed Larry stuffing spark plugs off the warehouse shelf into his jacket. He stared intently at the screen, then suddenly smiled in recognition. "Cool, that's me," he said without thinking.

Mrs. DeVincent-Milo stopped the film. "That, my fine friend, is your one-way ticket to the state penitentiary."

Larry slowly lowered his head down. A sudden thought bounced off some of the drug damaged neurons in his brain. Shit, I'm screwed.

Claire's sneer melted into an evil smile as she continued, "Unless you take care of something for me."

Headquarters - Parma City PD

Downey and her sergeant reported to the staff meeting and made their presentation. Denise felt like everyone attending was distracted and basically ignoring her. She asked if anyone had any questions. No one responded. A bad sign.

Assistant Chief Turner finally broke the stony silence and spoke up, "Thanks Detective. We will consider your recommendation for a specialized temporary task force and will advise you what we decide." He looked around the room. "Ladies and gentlemen, we will be adjourning for the rest of the morning. Please be back here at 1:00 PM for the community policing meeting."

Chief Milton stood, "I want to see Captain Brown and the assistant chiefs in my office for a few minutes, please. We will be having a briefing on that other matter."

Unsure of what to do, Downey looked at her sergeant who merely gestured for her to follow him out of the conference room.

In the elevator she asked him, "Are they always that weird?"

Sergeant Garver lifted his hands, palms up. "They're always weird, but never that weird. It must have something to do with the deal at the Mayor's office."

"What deal?"

"Oh, some vandalism or something. You know how the people at City Hall get when something happens. I'm going to go out, grab a newspaper and have a cup of coffee. I need to get out of here for a while. Do you want to come?"

Downey nodded, 'Sure, I definitely need to gear down from all this crap this morning. I've been stressing all week over it."

"Good, I'll buy."

CHAPTER 20

Police Headquarters
Bailey was flagged in like a fighter coming down on a carrier deck by the Chief's secretary pointing him into the boss's office. He was shocked that he didn't have to deal with the mandatory wait in the hall. He was even more shocked to see his Captain and two assistant Chiefs sitting in the office waiting for him with Milquetoast.

"Lieutenant, perhaps you can explain what happened to the media blackout on this thing," Milquetoast blurted out as Bailey came through the door. The Chief was shaking the morning edition of the Parma City Tribunal.

Bailey slowly reached for the paper and read the headlines. He stepped back. He grabbed his chest and considered faking a heart attack, until suddenly he realized he might actually be having a heart attack.

The headline on the front page read:
'PUBLIC OFFICIALS UNDER TERRORIST THREAT FOLLOWING GUN BATTLE NEAR CITY HALL.'

The finer print said something about militia groups, cover-ups, and the smoking ban in public buildings.

Bailey tried to think fast, "Uh - uh - uh." He looked back down at the headlines, "Holy shit."

Chief Lyle 'Milquetoast' Milton stood up with his arms crossed behind his back and accusingly asked Bailey what he knew about the media leak.

"Chief, I assure you, I don't have any idea where this information came from." He looked around the room for a friendly face but didn't see one. "Chief, this isn't even close to what happened. I can't imagine what kind of retard could even think something like this up."

Milton wasn't impressed. He started shaking. "You have plenty of potential suspects in that mob you supervise at SIU. It's those damned SCAT guys isn't it?" His face turned red with rage. Not a good sign. "Those assholes are trying to destroy the police department!" His eyes were starting to bulge. Worse sign.

Bailey was taken aback by the Chief's sudden burst of honest revelation. Everybody knew he was afraid of the SIU people. Now, he as much as admitted that he hated their guts, possibly as much as the SIU people hated his.

"Chief, be logical. My guys wouldn't want media attention focused on the events of last night any more than you do."

Captain Brown butted in, "He has a point, Chief. As weird as those people are at SIU, I can't even begin to think of anybody who could think up a story that ridiculous. Besides that, the paper identifies its source as someone inside City Hall."

Milton's shoulders drooped in surrender, "You're right of course. Even Bailey's people aren't that stupid." He looked across his desk at Bailey, "I want a solid lead on this case in 48 hours or you're back in a patrol car shaggin' calls."

Bailey thought that didn't sound bad.

"As a sergeant."

Bailey knew he couldn't handle the pay cut so he nodded in agreement and left the room. His pleasant mood from the morning had suddenly become a distant memory.

***

Bailey drove around town trying to chill out. One more cluster and that's it. I'll quit and sell shoes or something.

His cell phone rang and he flipped it open with a flick of the wrist.

"Yeah."

"Lieutenant?" It was the voice of Sergeant Mick Delgado.

"Yeah." I wonder what went wrong now?

"We need you at 50 West Juniper Street. Meth Lab."

Bailey felt like he had to puke. "Cooking?"

"Nah, cooked. It blew up."

"Damn! No kidding? What happened?"

"Looks like the chemist dozed off from inhaling the fumes and the ether ignited."

"Wow! Anybody hurt?"

"Actually, Boss, there are three dead bikers up here."

"No way, we're never that lucky. Are they the Devil's Thirteen club?"

"As far as we can tell right now, they were human, the only reason I called them bikers is because there's three melted Harleys out front."

Bailey groaned, "They fried the bikes? Bummer. I hate to see an innocent motorcycle pay the ultimate price for some assholes lack of common sense."

"You got that right, Skipper," the sergeant wholeheartedly agreed.

"I'll be there in fifteen minutes."

Archwald's Office

Slim Archwald sat at his desk trying to imagine the best way to capitalize on the current turn of events. Any intelligent person could see there was only one thing he could do in this situation. At midnight, he would take a crap on his desk.

As always, he methodically made up a check list of what to do and when to do it. He was methodical in that way. His mind working quickly, he rubbed his eyes and tried to envision what needed to be done. For sure, he would have to make an anonymous call to the press. He would need a note to tie it in to the other case. What did that note say? Something about a King? Oh well, add 'Call the Chief' to the list and get the wording on the note down correctly. Of course, a fake break-in. Almost forgot. That would be easy. Just break a window before he left. He smiled as he leaned back in his leather executive chair. Next step, Mayor's office. Mayor Archwald, then Senator Archwald. That sounds just fine.

Meth Lab

Bailey wheeled up to the curb and parked out of the way of the fire trucks. Lieutenant Beltron and Detective Tryon from homicide stood on the sidewalk pulling on protective lab clothing.

Frank saw Delgado and two of his detectives interviewing a neighbor. He got their attention and waved them over to meet with the homicide investigators.

Beltron took the first shot, "Frank, out checking on your undercover animals today?"

"I was heading over to the donut store to check on your bunch of loafers Fred. My guys are solving this dead bikers case for you clowns."

Delgado reached out to shake hands with Frank after the mandatory banter over which crew worked the hardest.

The other SIU detectives gathered around and Bailey began, "Victim identification?"

Delgado answered "Yeah, the president and two wanna-bees, crispy critters."

Beltran added, "Looks like cause of death, in laymen's terms is 'blown to smithereens'. These losers were making a batch of methamphetamine and apparently just got careless."

Tryon pointed to a scorched tree-top. "See that lump?"

Bailey nodded.

"That was the watch dog. I interviewed the maggot who owned this dump on a homicide investigation last year, and he threatened to turn that pit bull loose on me. I damn near shot the son-of-a-bitch but he was on a chain."

Bailey answered, "Yeah, with all these animal rights assholes around, it wouldn't look to good to shoot a chained dog."

Tryon corrected him, "Not the dog, the biker, some weird sex thing I interrupted."

Delgado looked up at the dog, "Damn, three dead bad guys and one dead bad dog, not to shabby of an afternoon's work if you ask me.

"Did the State Patrol meth lab guys show up yet?" Bailey inquired.

"Yeah, they wandered around in their space suits, filled out over-time slips and left. They declared it a lab explosion too. I guess that makes it legal."

Bailey answered, "All they really do is certify it eligible for federal funds to eliminate the toxic waste, otherwise the city would be on the hook for about fifty to a hundred grand for clean-up. These meth labs are an environmental nightmare."

Lieutenant Beltran let out a low whistle, "I'm glad we're not paying it."

Bailey laughed, "Where do you think the federal clean-up funds come from? You pay it pal, one way or the other."

Beltran frowned, "Shit."

Bailey stuck his hands in his pockets, "If there isn't anything else to do, I'm gonna make like a sheepherder and get the flock out of here."

The other detectives agreed.

Bailey shouted over his shoulder as he walked to his car, "Tag 'em and bag 'em Mick, throw a copy of the report on my desk. Thanks."

Bailey could see Delgado wave in acknowledgment out of the corner of his eye.

CHAPTER 21

Police Headquarters

Across town in the Chief's office, Milton was trying to do his usual job of making all the politicians happy and as usual, failing miserably. He held his chin in his hands as he studied his autographed picture of Jimmy Carter hanging on the wall behind his desk, and wondered what Old Grits would do in this situation. He had no answers.

Milton decided to phone the City Manager and ask him what to do. That was a safe call. You can't do the wrong thing if you're doing what the boss tells you.

Milton dialed the direct line to Gilmore's office.

The voice came on the line with a harsh, "Gilmore. I hope it's important."

"Sir, this is Chief Milton, I was just thinking about getting your opinion on our investigation into this terrorist thing."

"So far I haven't seen much of an investigation to form an opinion on. I certainly hope you have something for me to tell the council members, Chief."

Milton stammered. Maybe calling wasn't such a good idea. "Well... we are... I mean, I am..."

The edge on Gilmore's voice sharpened, "You are taking some sort of immediate action, aren't you Chief? Or do I have to run the police department myself?"

Milton cupped his forehead on his palm and stared at his desk in panic. He saw the proposal from the morning briefing on his desk and quickly formed the germ of an idea. "No, sir. I have an action plan right here that I have been working on, a little idea I came up with this morning."

***

Downey and Garver approached the intersection of Center and Southern when a call came over the radio announcing a disturbance at La Fuentés Bar, just a few blocks away near Parma Drive.

They looked at each other, smiled, and nodded in silent agreement that this call might far exceed the medical benefits of a coffee break. LaFuentés was a gay bar, notorious for fights. A little action might clear up the bureaucracy blues.

Denise cleared radio. "S-1227 and D-5494 are responding to the disturbance call, ETA two minutes.

Garver whipped through traffic and stomped the accelerator.

They slid into the parking lot, Starsky and Hutch style, bailing out before the car came to a complete halt.

Denise saw four of what could be men, two of which were dressed like women, duking it out in front of the entrance. A bartender, a very effeminate bartender, was running in circles screaming.

Denise pulled her pepper spray out of her pocket and shouted over the cacophony of sissies slugging it out.

"Knock it off, assholes, Police Officers."

The combatants ignored her and continued slapping, biting and kicking each other.

The Sarge bellowed in his deepest voice, "Police, freeze!"

The fighters ignored him, but the bartender, dressed in a baggy sleeved silk shirt and tight shorts that exposed his hairy muscular legs, walked over to the detectives with an exaggerated wiggle of the buttocks and began yelling.

"If you pigs don't do something this minute, I'll slap your faces! I mean it!"

Denise and her sergeant made eye contact and established a form of telepathy common in police work. They both knew this asshole was going to jail without speaking a word.

Denise stuck the pepper spray canister in the bartender's face and gave him the two second burst that she learned in training. She counted in her head, "One Mississippi, the scenic southern state and home of southern chivalry, Two Mississippi, with a mild climate and thousands of acres of cotton fields."

She painted the bartenders face with the spray and stepped back as he did a little agony dance before falling on his back, kicking in a circle like a Three Stooges routine.

The Sarge gave her a wink of approval as the swarm of patrol cars started rolling up.

Sergeant Deeson stepped out of one of the cars and ran up to assist Downey and Sergeant Garver with the remaining fighters.

Downey, struggling to cuff a suspect, looked over her shoulder to see Deeson push one of the suspects, a six foot-four transsexual wearing a plaid mini-skirt, against a car and begin to frisk him without cuffing him first.

Downey shouted, "Deeson, NO!"

She was too late. The cross dressing suspect shook his hips in a practiced wiggle causing his underwear to fall around his ankles, then waited. As Deeson squatted down to check the suspect's patent leather Go-Go boots for weapons, the suspect quickly spun around and hit the unsuspecting sergeant across the side of the head with his erect penis. An unusually large penis at that. The suspect's organ hit Deeson across the face with a loud SMACK, causing all arriving cops, suspects and onlookers to stop and stare in silence, not unlike when a teacher slams a ruler on a desk in a roomful of rambunctious kids.

Deeson froze in horror, a big red penis welt raised across the side of his face.

The suspect struck a vogue pose, "I hope that was good for you too, sweet cheeks!"

Deeson screamed in rage and reached for his gun. A patrol lieutenant and another officer jumped on him and pulled him back as the suspect turned an ran like a sprinting penguin leading a bayonet charge with his underwear still around his ankles.

The fleeing cross dresser made the mistake of watching over his shoulder at the screaming Deeson instead of where he was going and darted head-on into Officer Jeff Henderschott who gracefully stepped to the side, grabbed a handful of hair and promptly applied a carotid artery neck restraint choking the fleeing cross-dresser into unconsciousness.

Deeson, screaming profanities and threatening revenge on his assailant, struggled with the giggling officers who were trying to restrain him.

As the action subsided, half of the day-shift patrol division had arrived on the scene snickering at the red wiener welt on Deeson's kisser, as they arrested and cuffed the remaining suspects.

The Patrol Lieutenant in charge of day-shift gathered Garver, Downey and Henderschott into a loose huddle as he tried to piece together what had happened.

"Jeff, isn't a neck restraint a near deadly force option?"

"Sorry, Boss, but judging from the size of that damned thing, if what he did to Deeson wasn't assault on an officer with a deadly weapon, I don't know what is. Besides, I wasn't about to let that asshole smack me up side the head with his schlong."

"I see your point." The Lieutenant turned his attention to Downey and Garver. "I thought you folks were sex crimes detectives, not bouncers."

Garver pointed towards the scene of cross-dressers, flaming gays, and cops meandering around the parking lot. "If that isn't a sex crime, I'll kiss your... Ah hell." Garver decided to shut up before he dug himself in any deeper.

The Lieutenant looked over the scene, and sadly considered how he was going to write up this event summary.

"I guess I see your point too. I just hope this fiasco wasn't motivated by bias against this... alternative lifestyle." The Lieutenant didn't really care if it was or not, he was just preparing himself to answer the questions he knew would be coming from his captain, who happened to be gay.

Downey fielded this one, " Gosh Lieutenant, what alternate lifestyle are you referring to?" She batted her long eyelashes at him innocently, laying on her West Texas accent exceptionally thick.

The old patrol lieutenant shook his head and walked away muttering loud enough for Downey to make out, "Gay captains, gay suspects, assault with a deadly pecker, and cops who look like Barbie Dolls. Screw it, I'm out of here, I'm going to personnel and file my retirement papers."

Garver and Downey sat in their car writing supplements. They turned their paperwork over to Henderschott to attach to the patrol report before continuing on to their coffee break. At least now they had something interesting to talk about.

CHAPTER 22

Friday afternoon
DeVincent-Milo Car Dealership
President's office

"You want me to do what?'

"I don't want you to do it, I want you to hire someone to do it. I want to be sure that nobody can tie me to this thing. If you mention my name to anyone... I turn in the spark plug tape and you go to the joint. No one will believe you." Claire sat back in her black leather executive chair and stared at the lot boy with disdain.

Larry stuttered with shock. "L - L - Lady, I don't believe this. I mean, I know some guys who do...You know... jobs, b-b-b but... Shit!"

She leaned forward and jabbed her finger at him.

"Just do it asshole. Making eight hundred dollars is better than getting arrested. Even a dumb-ass like you should be able to figure that one out."

She got up from her chair and walked around to the front of her desk and stood arrogantly in front of Larry, tapping the video tape on her palm like an old time cop tapping his nightstick.

Larry knew the old bitch had a point. And, she was substantially smarter than him or she wouldn't be rich. All he had to do was hire some other loser worse off than himself. Someone to take a serious dump on her desk. Larry stopped and shook his head. He began wondering if the whole thing was one of his drug induced hallucinations, so he pinched himself a couple of times for a reality check.

He calmed down and replied. "All right. I met some guys the other day. They might do it, or maybe know who will."

De Vincent-Milo perched herself on the edge of her desk crossing and uncrossing her legs as she spoke.

"I don't care who does it, I just want it done within two days or the tape goes to the cops." She leaned across the desk and grabbed an envelope. She handed it towards him then pulled it away as he reached for it. "Three hundred now to hire the guy with, then I'll give you five hundred when the job is done."

Larry shrugged in agreement. "Do I have a choice? Get fired and prosecuted or hire someone to shit on your desk and leave town with eight hundred dollars. I may not be real smart, but I can figure that one out."

She threw the envelope at him. "Just don't fuck it up."

CHAPTER 23

"You want me to do *what*?" Bailey was westbound on Broadway at Parma Drive when the Chief got him on his cellular.

"A task force, damn it, I want a task force." Milquetoast Milton was passing along his 'original' solution as approved by the City Manager.

"What do you mean, a task force?" Bailey wanted to pinch himself to make sure this wasn't a Keystone Beer flashback or something.

"I mean, I'm pulling in detectives from every unit and assigning them to the SIU. I am also getting a federal agent from the FBI hate crimes unit. She should be here tomorrow. We'll be getting some action going on this case now, by God!"

Bailey shook his head in astonishment. He had been planning to assign two detectives to the case until this stupid thing blew over. He could spare two guys and still avoid any serious cases being neglected. Still, giving up two guys to this nonsense was going to be a heavy impact on the unit's case load. Now a task force?

"Chief, do you really want to do that? Every detective in the police department is stretched so thin on investigative time now..."

"Obviously, Lieutenant," the Chief's voice acidly spilled out of Bailey's cell phone and into his inner ear, "You don't see the big picture!"

Bailey almost threw the phone out the car window. He hated the big picture. Only assholes and emperors could see it.

Milton wasn't through, and Bailey knew it. He mouthed the Chief's reply with him as it came through the phone. "Do I need to get another Lieutenant to handle this?"

***

Chief Milton wasn't sure if he would get a "no sir" or a "fuck you". This Bailey character was so high strung. He got a "No sir, I can handle it."

Milton rocked back in his executive chair and winked at old Jimmy's picture on the wall. By God, I'll show 'em who knows how to run a damned investigation! He gave Bailey the news. "I'm glad you decided to get with the program. There will be a briefing with the press and the task force tomorrow morning at 10:00 A.M."

"I thought you wanted a press blackout?" Bailey asked.

Milton rolled his eyes at Bailey's question, who does this moron think he is? He damned sure wasn't command material.

"Of course not. We are a community based police department, Lieutenant. I have nothing to conceal from our friends in the press."

Bailey hit the mute button on the phone. "Asshole." He released the button and replied, "Yes sir, I'll be there with my men. I'm going to get some rest, then I'm going to be in tonight with the troops."

***

As Milton disconnected the Lieutenant he overheard the Chief's secretary say that Slim Archwald was on the line. Bailey cursed when he realized the Chief would bone him later, if he remembered it, for cutting out to get some rest rather than working twenty or thirty hours straight. Oh well, screw that asshole.

***

CHAPTER 24

Rowdy and Snort were heading for the 'All You Can Eat Spaghetti Lunch' special at Pedro Hirosata's diner on the corner of Southern and Park Drive. Pedro, or Pete to the SIU guys, was a friend of Bailey's, and he always made sure Frank's boys got good helpings of chow. The 'All You Can Eat Spaghetti' was a particular favorite of the SCAT team, with the plates full of steaming pasta and Pedro's special Japanese-Mexican sauce, thick with unknown, but tasty stuff. Just the fuel for crime-fighting machines.

Snort pulled into a Circle K to grab some smokes before they went to Pedro's. He got out of his tow truck and was walking toward the door when he saw a familiar figure squatting down by the phones, apparently waiting for a call.

"Hey, you're that dude from this morning." Snort let go with a baritone belch as he said it. Stomach acid from the thought of the spaghetti.

Larry flinched in surprise when he saw Snort, then he froze. It must be divine intervention, he thought. Nobody in the world will return my calls and then this dude shows up. "DUDE!" Larry sprang to his feet.

"Hey chill out asshole, I ain't your butt buddy here." Snort was put off by the sudden friendly enthusiasm of the dirt bag lot boy. He looked a little light in the loafers for Snort's taste.

"Oh man, am I glad to see you!" Larry babbled something about a job.

Snort was ignoring the street maggot, figuring he was going to hit him up for some money, when he heard the magic words, "Shit on a desk."

Snort looked around for witnesses. Seeing none, he grabbed Larry by the collar, threw open the passenger door on the tow truck and shoved the trembling lot boy into the seat between himself and Rowdy. "You want me to do what?"

"Look, it's a job, man. All you got to do is break into a place and take a shit on a desk. I'll get you fifty dollars. That's good money for ten minutes work."

"I might be a hit man, but not a shit man. What kind of job is taking a dump?" The cops gave themselves a psychological edge by both slowly leaning with all their weight into Larry causing him to feel the squeeze.

"It's my boss. That old bitch from the car dealership. I got the money from the other guys, and we want the job done. Is that a big deal? I thought you guys were players."

Snort grabbed Larry with his big left paw and squished his face. "Look you little fucker, don't get froggy with me or I'll take a shit right now and use you to wipe my ass!"

Rowdy, always the visionary, interrupted, "Wait a minute, you get us a hundred bucks and we'll get somebody who is a real pervert to do it. I know just the guy." He looked at Snort and winked, "Get the money and we'll bring the guy here at six o'clock tonight."

Larry was at a loss, "Yeah, I can do that."

Snort opened the door and pulled Larry out by the arm. "You had better fuckin' be here, asshole. If I hear you gave this job to somebody else, I'm gonna be fuckin' pissed off."

Larry brushed at his arm where Snort grabbed him trying vainly to rub away the pain. "I'll be here, no problem."

Snort backed out of the lot and headed back for Pedro's. "Are you thinkin' what I think you're thinkin', Rowdy?"

The Rowdy One placed his index finger on the Band-Aid between the lenses and pushed his glasses back on his nose. "Quintero."

Snort looked at his cerebral partner in admiration, "I wish I would have thought of that crazy bastard. I know he'll do it. The goofy fucker will probably insist on doing it."

Rowdy looked smugly ahead, " I would venture to guess that there will be steaming crap on the old bitch's desk tonight!"

***

Bailey pulled into his parking spot and shuffled to his front door. Tired as he was, he decided to give Denise a call. She should be at her desk by now. He threw down his bag of equipment and flopped on his couch grabbing the phone as he landed. He quickly punched in her number.

"Sex crimes, Detective Downey." The voice came across as all business, definitely not caring if you have a nice day or not.

"Hi, it's me." Bailey smiled as he imagined her heart rate accelerating at the sound of his voice, her face flushing with the recollection of the night before, the softening of her voice at the sound of her dream guy's call.

"Fuck you, asshole!"

Bailey sat up in shock, "No baby, it's me, Frank."

"I know who you are you dickhead. What's the idea of dumping my fucking proposal for some bullshit 'get-ahead-with-the-boys-downtown' case? Are you a cop or a politician? For God's sake Frank, this is an important deal. How could you do this to me?"

She took a breath and he dived in with the best defense he could come up with after her unexpected tirade, "Huh?"

"Don't ever call me again you 'suck-up piece of shit!" She punctuated the call with a receiver slam that hurt Frank's ear.

He stared at the phone as he set the receiver down. "I guess a blow job is out of the question."

***

Sergeant James was at home watching a western on T.V. when he got the call from Snort. "Sarge, I got something on the phantom shitter deal, but I think we're going to need some help."

James grabbed his bottle of Maalox that he kept by the phone for these type of calls from the guys. He guzzled about half a bottle and asked the question, "This ain't illegal is it?"

"No, Sarge. Some asshole wants to hire a guy to take a shit on somebody's desk. I think we ought to go for it. It's just too coincidental with the deal down town."

James had to consider what crime might be involved. "What kind of charge do we have if we take the contract?" He sure missed his thousand 'cc' Kawasaki and motor boots. The young babes loves the guys in those breeches and motor boots. Best of all, when you wear the helmet, they can't tell that you're bald.

Snort broke into the reverie with a list of charges that Rowdy had written on one of Pedro's napkins during their dinner break. "I think it's conspiracy for burglary, criminal damage to property, a health code violation, and maybe even some kind of terrorist thing or something."

James hated approving weird stuff but it went with the job description of SIU supervisor. "Go ahead and get the ball rolling, and we'll brief it tonight when the Lieutenant gets in." He added as an afterthought, "What was the help you're going to need?"

There is no way to break bad news other than to come right out with it, so Snort sucked up his guts and just said it, "We'd like to get Quintero assigned back over to SIU to be the shit man."

James felt sweat break over his forehead in a bead where his hairline used to be. His stomach turned over. He grabbed the Maalox and finished the bottle. "You want to do WHAT?"

"Sarge, he's the only one I know of who will actually do it if necessary. And he's the only guy I know who looks like he would take a dump on somebody's desk for money."

"For money?" James nerves frayed further as he remembered the days of Bailey, Quintero, and himself working undercover together as detectives. "That asshole would do it for free." James thought fast, "Besides that, he said he would never leave patrol again." The old sergeant had to know, "Is he still checking off for lunch at the mortuary parking lot?"

"Sarge, he's not that weird anymore. Please, we want to use him on this."

"Didn't he report to briefing in a dress as a tribute to Dennis Rodman last month?"

"Sarge, you got to admit, Dennis Rodman is one hell of a rebounder."

James was frightened that the response had made some sort of sense to him. "I don't think Bailey will clear it, but check it out and see if he's available." James hung up the phone and checked his liquor cabinet. He needed a drink.

On the street
Patrol Officer Quintero stopped at a phone booth in response to a page. He wiped his shaved head with an old towel he kept in his patrol car. He dialed the number and answered Snort's impatient "yeah" with the lifeless, monotone, eerily demented voice of a psychiatric patient with way too much Thorazine in his system.

"This - is - Thomas - Q. - Quintero."

"Dude, it's Snort..."

Quintero listened to Snort's story. "You want me to do what?" Quintero laughed uncontrollably in his strange 1940's monster movie villain laugh. "Of course, I'll do it," He replied in the scary baritone followed by more scary laughter. "But first, let me check with Mr. Pepé." Quintero looked at the little face painted on the base of his right index finger and formed a little mouth with his thumb.

"Mr. Pepé, shall Quintero shit on a council member's desk in the line of duty?"

Quintero made a squeaky little voice for Pepé's response, "No Quintero, you swore never to go back to SIU!"

He deepened to his baritone, "But I must, my department needs me, the people need me, Bailey needs me!"

The little voice returned, "Fuck Bailey!"

Quintero broke from his conversation to glare at a little kid sitting in the passenger seat of a passing car, laughing at the policeman talking to his hand. The youngster quickly turned away and slid down the seat out of sight.

Quintero continued, "Pepé, don't make me force you to wrestle the snake again!"

Quintero heard a click as the line disconnected and he let out with another of his strange deep laughs again.

Back at the SIU offices, Snort slammed the phone and looked over his shoulder at Rowdy, standing behind his chair listening in on the conversation. He put his hands on his forehead. "What have I done? Dear God, what have I done?"

Rowdy pushed his glasses back again, "I would hazard to guess that we fucked up royally!"

Snort lit a cigarette, "No horse shit." A twisted smile distorted his features, "But, I think life around here is going to get a little more interesting."

Snort pushed himself out of the chair and both detectives shouted, "SCAT Team!" and bumped chests like the sports heroes they believed they were. In the game of maggot ass-kicking, they were the MVPs.

***

CHAPTER 25

Police Headquarters

Briefing started at sixteen hundred hours. Bailey hadn't been able to get any rest after being blasted by Denise. Sergeant Hank James hadn't been able to get any rest after the call from Snort. Rowdy and Snort seemed irritable at the possibility of having bitten off more than could be chewed with the Quintero recruitment. The other Special Crimes and Apprehensions Team (SCAT) guys made small talk waiting to get started.

Sergeant James took Bailey by the arm. "Sir, there is something going on that you need to hear about, alone."

Bailey melted into a slouch and whined, "Do I have to know?"

"Believe me Lieutenant, you want to know." He briefed the boss on Larry the maggot, Snort, and the contract on the poop job.

"That might actually be something. I think we should do it." Bailey was relieved at finally getting a break on this damned thing.

"Sir, that's not all. The guys think we should bring in some extra help on this thing."

"Whoa, small world. Milton told me he's bringing in quite a bit of extra help. Sounds good to me, what do they want to do?"

James told him.

"They want to do what?" Bailey consciously tried to restrain his rage. "Anything... Anything but that moron Quintero. Did you know he was written up last month for standing on top of the freeway overpass, in uniform with a black cape, yelling over a bullhorn that he was Quintero the Magnificent, God's answer to crime? I mean, what the hell does that mean, God's answer to crime? He's over the edge. Way over. No way."

Hank James was nodding in agreement injecting an "I know, I know" whenever he could. He finally stopped Bailey's ranting. "Look Frank, do you want this phantom shitter thing to end? I know I do. Who else do you know who looks like he is capable of breaking into an office and taking a dump on a desk. I mean, not everybody has that kind of charisma."

"Yeah, but the phantom shitter already does it. I can't believe this is really related."

Hank put his hand on the Lieutenant's shoulder, "Frank, you and I both know the phantom shitter is most likely a disgruntled employee doing a one-shot revenge thing. It will probably never happen again. If we go out and make a bust on this Larry guy, the bosses will be satisfied that we cleared the case and it's all over. This is a win-win situation."

Bailey had to agree with his logic. In a political case, like this one, the brass only cares that someone, somewhere went to jail for something so they can get the press off their back. It might work.

Bailey took a deep breath and paused. "Hank, if you think it's such a good idea, and I ain't saying it's not, you can do it."

Sergeant Hank James smiled.

Bailey continued, "But you're responsible for that lunatic Quintero. Whatever he does, you pay for."

Sergeant Hank James frowned.

"Look Hank, After the... incident. That shooting. He has gotten even crazier. He swore he would never work undercover again and I... That whole deal was my screw-up. I just don't want anything else to go wrong."

Hank James nodded, "I know. And if it wasn't for that crazy bastard, you and I wouldn't be around today having this conversation. I'll watch him the best I can."

Bailey returned to the briefing room. "Troops, I think you should know that a task force is being formed to deal with this current situation."

A detective asked, "Do you mean Downey's pervert surveillance?"

"Ah, no. The alleged terrorist surveillance. The sex crime case was deemed too weak for the investment in manpower. We will be working on the matter of persons unknown trying to intimidate the local government representatives." Bailey paused at the sound of general snickering. "It is getting a little crazy, I know. But please give it your best shot and this too shall pass."

He turned the briefing over to James, who put the operational plan on the board for the meeting with Larry.

As James was writing on the board, a young detective raised his hand. "Sarge, are we actually going to have to go through with a court ordered break-in and the defecation. I'm not sure, but I thought a conspiracy wouldn't fly without an overt act."

James tried to act astonished, "A court ordered break-in to plant a listening device falls under the President's new anti-terrorist legislation. We won't need the overt act under those statutes." He took a deep breath and lied, "I'm virtually certain we won't have to do the...defecation to complete the sting operation."

Suddenly, the back door to the briefing room slammed open, stilling all conversation in the room. A shaved headed, caped figure wearing ragged denim jeans and sporting a tank top that said "Kill a Commie for Mommy" stepped in and strode over to Bailey. He stood facing the Lieutenant for a moment then grabbed Bailey's ears and said, "I love you, white boy." Then he tried kissing him on the mouth.

Bailey pushed him away screaming, "Get away from me you homosexual asshole." Then Bailey started spitting on the carpet, "Phtew, phtew—James-phtew," Bailey pointed at his sergeant with a threatening gesture. "You're responsible for this asshole!"

Quintero stopped in the center of the room full of wide-eyed young narcs. "Yes I am a homosexual. So what. I'm also a bi-sexual and a tri-sexual. I like sheep and chickens too. Ha, ha , ha , ha, ha." Quintero laughed his scary monster laugh. He raised his hand to reveal the little face drawing to the detectives, "Mr. Pepé likes to spank the donkey, ha, ha, ha, ha!"

Snort stood up, holding his Harley-Davidson Baseball cap in his hands, and addressed the young wide-eyed detectives in the room like a sheepish academy award recipient, "You know, I just wanted to take this opportunity to say it's a pleasure to see you, and Sarge and the Lieutenant finally working together again after all these years." He looked around the room at the confused group of narcs, "This is kind of like a historic moment for the SIU and the SCAT Team, I wish you would all join me in a moment of silence."

Rowdy bowed his head and started singing an off key version of Amazing Grace. He only knew the words 'Amazing Grace' and repeated them over and over to the familiar tune as the other detectives joined in.

Bailey put his hands up in front of his face, "I think I'm going to puke."

Hank, the peacemaker, jumped between the Lieutenant and the troops. "We can take it from here, Skipper. Why don't you go out back and have a smoke until we get the ball rolling. I'll page you."

The Lieutenant grabbed his friend by the sleeve, "Hank, if Quintero turns this into any more of a circus than it is right now, I don't care if the crazy bastard did save both our lives, I'm going to shoot him. And then I'm going to shoot you. Then I'm going Postal on the whole friggin' place. And I'm saving the last round for myself!" Bailey stomped off to the elevator, still spitting and rubbing his mouth with his sleeve.

Hank James talked to no one but himself, "I miss traffic division. This kind of shit never happens there."

***

The Mayor enjoyed an evening of sitting at home in front of the TV watching Wheel of Fortune. He couldn't guess the answer to anything anymore but, boy that Vanna was hot. He finished his cream of wheat and fell asleep in his favorite chair.

He woke up to the sound of a ringing phone. A telephone solicitor asked him if he was the home owner. The Mayor couldn't remember if he was or not and hung up. Wondering whose house he had been sleeping in.

Across Town

At Slim Archwald's land development office, a figure in dark clothing sneaked around the alley to the back door and entered with a key. Archwald had been at home drinking prune juice until dark, waiting for the mood to overtake him. He knew that he would be nervous faking the break-in and might not be able to go. He thought of himself as an individual who was always prepared, just a little smarter than the local constabulary, the bunch of civil service losers.

He carried an OD green duffel bag containing toilet paper, a back-up bottle of prune juice, and the note he printed on his computer based on the information the Chief had given him.

He could hear the music to 'Mission Impossible' playing in his head as he moved with as much stealth as possible down the hall to his office slithering through the corridors with his back to the wall, anxiously peering left and right through the darkness.

He looked up and down the hallway leading to his office suite, then entered. He moved quickly. He wanted to be sure they found the note, so he pulled off a piece of adhesive tape and attached it to the back of his chair. He climbed up on the desk, dropped his sweat pants, squatted in a position like a constipated gargoyle, and tried to go. He tightened up once, twice, then felt his bowels surge. His expression of grim satisfaction suddenly turned to panic as 'it' happened. The prune juice took full effect and he lost control. He did a little frog dance with his sweat pants around his ankles mouthing, "Aaah, aaah, aaah," as the foul smelling diarrhea flowed over the desk, his shoes, and his pants.

He tried to stop himself, but couldn't. As he struggled his feet went out from under him and he fell off the desk striking his head on a bronze bust of himself as he toppled to the floor, killing him instantly.

***

CHAPTER 26

Denise Downey, sat in her truck and sipped coffee from the Styrofoam cup, working the kiddy porn cum child molest surveillance by herself. She smoldered in a slow burn as she thought about her request for a surveillance team being blown off because it didn't fit criteria for likely apprehension. Not cost effective. Bullshit!

Dingo was her man, the asshole behind the kiddy porn ring and her child molester.

She flipped through her file. Dingo was just the street name for the thirty-nine year old computer programmer. If it wasn't for the net chat lead, she wouldn't have found the two prior child molest convictions. Two convictions, she thought, and less jail time than a DUI. It was tough getting these guys taken down. Little kids are never good witnesses and juries have a hard time believing nice looking people can commit such an atrocity.

Denise caught herself grinding her teeth again. Her jaws were so tight, she had given herself another headache. "I got to get into another line of work." She whispered to no one. She rubbed her eyes and tried to imagine what a normal life would be like. Maybe life with Frank, if they weren't both damned cops maybe they could be normal, whatever the hell that was.

Her anger turned to guilt for coming down on Frank for stealing her plan. He didn't have anything to do with it. It was that asshole Milton and the scumbags on the City Council. They wanted to blow off this molester case in the interest of politics, so fuck 'em. She would do it herself, on her own time.

She put her cup down and settled back to watch from the cab of her pick-up truck outside the target's house. No more than a half an hour passed before she saw him pull in his driveway behind the wheel of a Cadillac bearing Arizona personalized license plate "DINGO".

Denise almost choked on her drink when she saw he had a little boy with him carrying a stuffed toy. Dingo kept nervously looking down the street and over his shoulder.

Downey's face contorted with rage. Dingo had no children and his probation agreement forbid him to be near or approach any children. "That son-of-a bitch abducted another kid." Her eyes teamed with anger, "God-damn it, Frank! You're never here when I need you." She sat alone, wondering what to do next.

***

Snort, Rowdy, and Quintero sat in the tow truck by the phone booth waiting for Larry to show up. Six o'clock came and went. They made small talk on the line-of-sight channel on the radio with Sergeant James who was covering them from across the street.

At 7:30 P.M. an obviously stoned Larry staggered up to the passenger side of the truck. He leaned with his hand against the cab and a slap happy expression in his eyes. He hadn't heard Snort exit the drivers side. He started to say something when he felt his face smash against the window.

"You're late, asshole." Snort hated to be kept waiting.

"Man, I'm sorry, I'm sorry. I got your money. Chill out." Larry was trembling and thought he might lose control of his bladder.

Snort kept Larry's face pressed against the glass. Quintero suddenly pressed his face against the other side of the glass, eye to eye with Larry, scaring him so badly he started screaming. Snort popped Larry's forehead against the glass smartly enough to get his attention and settle him down.

"Shut up you fucking worm!"

"Okay, okay. This must be the dude, cool. No problem." Larry tried to compose himself and Snort let him go.

Quintero exited the truck, "My associates tell me you need a 'job' done. Well, I'm the man." He threw his head back and sniffed the air.

Snort was a man to get to the point, "We're ready right now, just tell us where and we'll do it."

Larry couldn't get his head straight after a day of non-stop dope usage, but he felt compelled to do his best to cooperate with the strange looking bald guy and the big ugly biker. The other strange little guy was standing in the background pushing his thick eye glasses back on his nose.

"Okay. It's the car dealership I work at, you know the place, with that crazy bitch from the commercials. It's her office. There ain't no alarm so nobody should know, just take a healthy one on her desk and that's it."

Rowdy finally broke into the conversation, "I would like to know, why exactly are you forking over good money for someone to take a shit on your boss' desk?"

Larry tried to recall what the skinny guy's name was. "Hey, you look like that New York actor dude who wears the glasses and makes those movies nobody watches."

Snort shook him again, "Answer the question, shit for brains."

"Okay, okay. She wants it done, I don't fucking no why."

Snort raised his voice, "Who is 'she'?"

Larry appeared stunned that he let that part slip. "Aw shit." He started whining again, "Dude, I wasn't supposed to say that part, man, just forget it, all right?"

"No, it ain't all right." Quintero was taking his turn. "Either I know everything or - No shit."

"Look, here's the money, just take it and do the job. I don't want to get in any more trouble."

Snort's pager went off. He looked at it and saw the code 10*15 from his sergeant.

Snort looked at the other detectives, "That's the bust signal." He grabbed Larry without a word and threw him in the truck. Snort figured that the show of money must have been enough of an overt act for the conspiracy charge. The first part was easy. He wondered if James heard the part about the Council Lady being the contractor on this job.

***

Denise Downey made a decision. Not the simple kind that you make ever day about jobs, bills, or appointments. She decided to take justice into her own hands. At risk was her job and maybe prosecution. At stake was the safety and well-being of probably dozens of children and their families, not to mention that small boy. The dozens of children that it was likely Mr. Kiddy porn would molest in his lifetime. She set her jaw and spoke out loud, "I took an oath to protect and serve. I think it's time to do just that."

She pulled her Glock nine millimeter out of her fanny pack and exited the pick-up truck. She approached the suspect's house, staying in the shadows. Then she heard it. Her blood ran cold. A small child screamed.

***

The narcs tried to ignore Larry's incessant chattering from the little area he was stuffed in behind the front seat of the truck .

"I knew you bastards were cops. I knew it." He started crying as he wiggled around trying to get more comfortable. "I got rights! This is entrapment! I ain't talking."

Rowdy looked back at him over the seat, "We ain't asking you anything Larry, we think you're the ringleader and you're going down. We'll be big heroes and you'll be getting punked by some big Aryan Brotherhood guy in the joint. Everyone will live happily ever after." He paused. "Except for you, of course."

Larry quietly sniveled, "Can I have a cigarette?"

Quintero answered, "You'll earn enough of those in the joint getting butt-fucked. You'll be waking up with a bloody asshole, a cigarette, and a note from Bubba on your pillow saying thanks for the memories."

Larry started howling and whining like a dog that had been hit by a car, but the narcs ignored him for the rest of the trip to Headquarters.

Larry sat sniveling in a holding room in the Criminal Investigations Division at Headquarters. Rowdy had read him his rights and received a voluntary waiver.

Larry blurted between sobs, "I'll tell you guys everything, just let me the fuck out of here."

Rowdy flipped on a tape recorder and let Larry spill the whole scam on Claire De Vincent-Milo and her plan to have someone shit on her desk. The only thing he couldn't supply was the 'why'.

Rowdy closed out the interview and left Larry whimpering about his bad fortune in the little holding room. He found Hank James and laid the whole thing out. "Our only way to find out 'why' is to bring her in and cop her out, which I don't want to do, her being a council man or lady, or whatever. You know, we could go ahead and do the job, wire up Larry, then send him in maybe with Quintero to collect the money. Get the old bitch on tape, and her ass is ours."

Hank shook his head in disbelief. "This shit is political now, I better run it by the Lieutenant. You keep Larry on ice and all you assholes keep your fucking mouths shut."

***

CHAPTER 27

Denise stepped back and kicked the door twice with all her might before it sprang open. She raised her Glock to the combat ready position and began clearing the front room as her heart raced out of control. The small boy was prone face down on the floor with a pillowcase over his head and his hands and wrists secured with black electricians tape, the type used in the other molestation cases.

Then she saw him. Her attention and her gun zeroing in on Dingo, the child molester. The monster.

She drew down on him, "Police, FREEZE!"

The man turned. His trousers were undone and she could see he was obviously sexually aroused. Denise knew his kind, they get so wrapped up in their perversions they get tunnel vision, oblivious to everything around them but their victims.

"I said, POLICE, FREEZE!" She screamed as her adrenaline fired her senses to the extreme.

The suspect froze in surprise. "What?"

"Step away from that child, you fucking maggot!" Denise no longer saw Dingo, she saw another man, a man who had been physically dead for years, but was kept alive in the depths of her darkest nightmares, her terrible childhood terror.

Dingo started to regain his senses, "You can't come in here like that! Where's your fucking warrant? I know my rights!"

Denise's hands began shaking and her eyes welled with tears, "Fuck you, you worthless prick!" Her voice was strained and wavering. Memories she fought for almost thirty years to suppress flooded her mind.

The initial confidence faded from Dingo's tone, "What? What did you say?"

Her voice flattened. Calmly and slowly she replied, "I said, fuck you... You worthless fucking baby raping prick!"

Dingo grabbed the weeping child around the throat and pulled him up in front of him as a shield, "Get back or I'll break this little bastard's neck!"

Denise asked him, "Have you ever heard that saying, life's a bitch?" Her voice became suddenly calm and her hands steady.

A look of confusion edged with panic etched his face. "Yeah, why?"

"Because for you... tonight... It damned sure is. And so am I."

Dingo stood frozen, eyes widening in realization. He stepped back in desperation, pushing the child away and started to raise his hands, then lunged forward, reaching for her gun.

She stepped back and to the left in a modified Weaver combat stance. Shooting for center mass, she repeatedly squeezed the trigger. She had never been a top shooter on the range during quarterly qualifications, but under stress she fought like she trained, remembering to focus on the front sight and stitching the suspect up the middle, walking the rounds up from his lower abdomen.

The semi-automatic jammed and she felt the slide lock back. Believing she had emptied the gun, she depressed the magazine release button causing the magazine to fall out of the grip as she pulled a fresh one out of her belt and rammed it in. The force cleared the jammed round and the slide slammed forward.

He staggered from the rounds tearing open his bowels, but didn't fall. He used both hands to try and hold his guts in place as he screamed a curse at the detective. Denise took aim and fired one last round catching him squarely in his open mouth, snapping his head back and violently throwing him to the floor.

She stood over the body staring down at him as he stared up at her, eyes vacant. In her mind, she saw the face change from the animal who brutalized her as a child, to the face of the man whose actions had brought the memories back.

The body's legs reflexively twitched after death, as Denise, still in a trance-like state, slowly walked into the kitchen and opened drawers until she found a nice-sized steak knife. She picked it up with a tissue she pulled from her pocket and tossed the blade near the body.

Although she felt a calm she had never before experienced, she made a breathless call on the radio for an officer involved in a shooting, nine-nine-nine.

SIU Offices

Emma sat in the office, trying to catch up on late reports. She listened to the scanner from time to time just to break the monotony. She just leaned back in her chair to clear her head when she heard it come out over the patrol channel.

"D-5494. Nine, nine, nine, officer needs assistance, shots fired."

"Damn." She immediately recognized Denise's voice and call sign.

Emma was one of only a couple people who were aware of Bailey and Denise's on again, off again relationship. They took a lot of pains to keep things quiet realizing it wouldn't help either of their careers to advertise an office romance. But Emma was close enough to Bailey to know how he felt about Denise. She was one of the two people he confided in about them. She grabbed her purse and headed out the door. She knew she could find Bailey at Headquarters. She also knew he probably wouldn't be monitoring the patrol channel. She had better be there to take care of him. He would be a basket case.

***

Hank James heard the hot call come out over a nearby patrol officer's portable radio. He had been in the process of paging Bailey for clearance on going ahead with the undercover operation. The triple-nine call changed all that. James knew as soon as Bailey got word that Denise had been in a shooting, he wouldn't be able to function logically. Hank James was the other person who knew about the relationship between the old Lieutenant and the young sex crimes detective.

Hank shook his head in disbelief. "God-damn it, Bailey's out of it. I'm the man. Shit, I'm screwed." He spoke out loud to no one in particular, "Lucky for me I'm black. If this turns to shit, Milquetoast won't screw with me too much."

The nearby beat officer heard the old sergeant mumbling and looked at him with an expression of concern, "Sir?"

James waved him off, "Nothing, I was just saying that the Chief is afraid of colored folks." He wandered down the hall to give Snort the green light on the operation.

The confused patrol officer stood there for a few seconds, not sure how to respond. Finally he just said, "Oh." and walked away.

***

CHAPTER 28

Claire De Vincent-Milo sat in the booth of the Scottsdale night club with her young escort. Once she dressed him up, the young mechanic was really quite handsome. She chattered on about her sexual prowess causing her employee to squirm around nervously.

Claire felt particularly excited this evening, knowing that soon the newspapers would discover she was the target of political terrorism. Once that disgusting hippie took care of the contract, she would be on her way to the governor's office.

Claire often grabbed a young hunk out of the shop for a sexual celebration. For these indiscretions, her staff secretly referred to the mechanics' shop as the 'service center.'

Unfortunately for the naive selectees, she usually transferred them to her dealership in Gila Bend, fifty miles into the desert from Phoenix, shortly after the lurid affairs.

***

The young mechanic was unsure of how to respond to Claire's strange monologues.

"Just keep in mind, Bobby..."

"I'm Jim, ma'am."

"Whatever, I only have six rules about sex. I don't do animals, I don't do children, I don't do pain, maybe a little spanking, I don't do your friends, I don't do women, and I damned sure don't do dead guys."

"Dead guys?" His confused expression was overlooked by Claire. He excused himself to go to the bathroom and made a call to his uncle who operated a small garage in Tempe.

"Uncle Pete, do you still need a mechanic at the shop?... I'm interested, yeah...Great, can you do me a favor and pick me up at the corner of Scottsdale Road and Indian School?"

***

Rowdy got an order signed by a Superior Court judge to make the entry and plant a listening device. The judge had a sense of humor, and was of the opposite political persuasion as the politically active De Vincent-Milo.

With Larry in tow, Snort and Quintero quickly defeated the dead bolts on Claire's office building and scooted carefully down the hall toward her office.

Larry pointed out the door and they all stood in silence as Snort did the lock with his picks.

Quintero dramatically stepped into the center of the room, " Is this... the desk?" He spoke in halting monotone.

Larry nodded his head energetically.

Snort took a 'before' picture of the desk with his date-time camera. Then motioned for Quintero to do the deed.

Larry's eyes widened as Quintero stepped forward and started to undo his trousers. Larry backed up toward the door, "You sick fuckers!"

Quintero ripped loose with one of his extended monster laughs. "You fool! Quintero doesn't do shit for the man!" He reached into his black bag and pulled out a plastic box containing a fake fecal specimen prepared by Von Hammel at the lab. He placed the specimen squarely on the desk top and Snort took another picture. The detectives quickly replaced a wall socket with a disguised listening device and, after wiping off any potential fingerprints out of force of habit, left the premises.

***

CHAPTER 29

Bailey's knees went weak when Emma told him the news. "Is she okay?"

Emma held his hand, she could see his eyes slightly watering. Her eyes watered too as she saw the weight of concern crushing her friend, a friend who had seen the worst of humanity too many times. "I'm sure she's fine Frank. It just sounded serious and I wanted to make sure you didn't get surprised."

Frank ran a hand over his face and wiped off the window to his feelings. "Emma, will you check it out for me. I don't want to get over there and have a scene. The last I spoke to her... I don't think she wants to see me anyhow. She thinks I'm the asshole who stole her idea and took the manpower off the case she's on. And now look what's happened."

He looked composed, but suddenly he took a step and drop kicked a small wastebasket across the room. "THAT FUCKING PUSSY MILTON!" His rage leveled off again and this time was able to maintain control. " I'm sorry Emma, these people we work for are just... unbelievable."

Emma gave her boss a hug. "Chill out honey, what goes around comes around. I'll check on Denise and call you as soon as I know something."

Bailey hugged back. " Mutha, I don't know what I'd do without you." She looked in his face and saw he meant it.

***

Snort and Quintero shoved Larry into the truck and slowly drove out of the parking lot. Quintero grabbed the scrambled SIU radio, "The eagle has landed, I repeat, the eagle has landed."

James piped up on the air, "Secure that unauthorized traffic right now god-damn it!"

Snort forcibly took the radio away from Quintero, "Sir, we're clear. We're taking our 'cooperative individual' back to Headquarters."

Hank James responded, "Check, get some rest. I want you both in the monitoring room at zero-five hundred hours." Hank sat back in his chair. He thought to himself. What have I done?

***

The first officer on the scene came through the front door with his partner in the initial moves of a dynamic building entry. He found Detective Downey cradling a young boy, who was softly whimpering in her arms. The uniformed officers slowed to a stop and lowered their weapons from the combat position to the ready position.

Officer Jeff Henderschott, a ten year veteran, searched the room with his eyes. He pointed his Sig Sauer 220 at the body across the room. "Denise, is this the only asshole?"

She nodded.

Henderschott looked at his rookie partner, who was visibly shaken at the bloody corpse, "Scotty, I'd say this piece of shit is code four, he ain't gonna cause any more trouble." He ambled over to the body examining it with distaste. "Notify dispatch."

The rookie quickly left the house and began talking on the radio.

Jeff knelt down by Denise and put a comforting hand on her shoulder. "This is the guy who was hanging around the school yards in my beat, isn't it?" He knew more about the suspect, but he didn't want to say it.

Again, she nodded.

Henderschott stood up and offered her a hand. "Looks like the son-of-a-bitch brought a knife to a gun fight. Nice work, Downey."

She took the hand, then got up. While Henderschott started making notes, she walked to the door with her head down. Denise paused, then turned and handed her weapon to Henderschott. "Here, I think I'm supposed to give you this."

He accepted the weapon and stuffed it in the back of his gunbelt. He reached down into an ankle holster, drew his back-up piece and handed it to her. "Just in case."

She carried the child as she walked out to her car and waited for the circus to begin. Henderschott's partner started rolling crime scene tape and setting up a perimeter. Another officer took the child.

Emma was one of the first on the scene. She saw Denise and gave her a hug. "Are you going to be okay, Hon?" She didn't ask what happened because it really didn't matter to her.

"Emma." Her eyes filled with tears and she started to sob.

Emma took her by the arm and led her away from the arriving crowd. She stopped a short distance away and put her hands on Denise's shoulders. She stared her in the eyes.

"Baby, stop it. Don't let these guys see you being weak. I'll cry with you later, but not here. Get a grip." The words weren't the approved touchy-feely psycho-babble that police psychologists talked about today, but politically correct or not, it was the right thing to say.

Denise knew if the guys saw a young, female officer showing emotion after having to cap a maggot, she would hear about it the rest of her career. Denise bit her lip. She shook her head in agreement and wiped her face with a tissue. "You're right Emma, it's just..."

"I know." Emma squeezed her shoulder gently. "I'm going to call Frank. He's worried sick."

"Thanks, Emma." She said as they both walked back to the crowd of officers.

Emma dialed Bailey on her cell phone while she watched Denise briefing the Watch Commander. Frank picked it up on the first ring.

"What did you find out, is she okay?"

"She had to take some asshole out. She'll be okay. She didn't get hurt physically, but... There is going to be some real emotional scar tissue there."

"Holy shit."

"Frank, I'm going to give her some time to deal with the crowd and then I'll tell her to call you."

Frank closed his eyes. "Thanks, Emma."

The big red-head snorted, "You owe me, asshole!" She disconnected when she heard Bailey snicker at her response. Another mission accomplished by 'Mutha.'

On surveillance

At six o'clock the next morning, Snort, Rowdy and Quintero huddled around the speaker at the listening post, monitoring the activity in Claire De Vincent-Milo's office. They heard the door lock being fumbled with then muffled giggling. They turned the gain up on the volume, leaning closer to the speaker, straining to hear what was going on when Claire let loose with an unexpected piercing scream, "TERRORISTS! TERRORISTS! CALL THE NEWSPAPER AND THE POLICE!"

All three detectives danced on their toes around the room, holding their ears. "Bitch!" "Asshole!" "Bitch!" they cursed as Rowdy released one ear long enough to turn the volume back down.

The detectives settled back down and continued monitoring.

They could hear some employees enter the room while Claire continued to shriek about terrorists and calling some reporters.

They heard her phone go off hook, as she punched in a number.

"Editor, please." Claire waited for a few seconds then continued, " Jerry, you'll never believe what happened. The terrorists. They attacked me. Well no, not physically, they did the same thing as they did at City Hall. No, I don't know who they were. They had to be the same terrorists who attacked the Mayor... What do you mean, is that all they did? Jerry, you asshole, I'm trying to tell you that terrorists are after me for my political stand and I ain't backing down!... You know, my political stand against, uh... you know, different things."

The editor responded, "Tell me you're not referring to the stupid cigarette smoking ban you people passed over there. Or is it that photo-radar crap? Get a grip Claire, you people aren't progressive, you're annoying, and if someone defecated on your desk, its probably because of one of your shady used car deals! AND THAT AIN'T NEWS!"

The detectives were giggling at the flurry of curse words from Claire as the editor apparently hung up on her.

Snort looked at his two partners with satisfaction, "Time for phase three."

CHAPTER 30

Bailey got the call on his cell phone as he drove over to the SIU offices. "You did *what?*"

Hank James tried to make it sound like it was nobody's fault. "Lieutenant, things just started rolling and boom. There the stinking thing was."

"Hank, I don't want to talk about this on the cellular. Get over to the office and leave the three amigos... wherever they are."

Bailey massaged his left temple, "Moe-Rons". He thought about it while he drove through light traffic. It was too crazy to get pissed off. Snort, Rowdy, and his goofball ex-partner Quintero broke into a council person's private office and planted feces on her desk in order to catch the suspect who did it to the Mayor. Shit! I'm getting fired.

SIU Offices

At four in the morning, Bailey made some coffee while James ran a cordless electric shaver over his face. They sat down in Bailey's office. James flopped over the ugly little love seat that Bailey had rescued from a dumpster last year. Bailey propped his feet on the desk and leaned back in the office chair. They both stared silently at the large poster of John Wayne hanging over Bailey's metal bookcase.

The Duke sat on a big appaloosa stud, looking over his shoulder at the two burned-out supervisors. Bailey wondered what the 'Big Man' would do in this situation. In a moody daze Bailey tried a John Wayne imitation, "I wouldn't try that, pilgrim."

James sat up and looked at Bailey, "Who are you calling a pilgrim?"

"Ahh, settle down, I was just thinking out loud."

"Well, you know if John Wayne was here, he would have done the same thing I did."

Bailey snorted, "I'm sure. Duke was always known for having some guys break into a place and take a dump on somebody's desk."

"That ain't what I mean." He moved to the edge of the couch. "I know you're worried about Denise. It ain't your fault. Milton is the retard that pulled the other guys from her unit to ours. She's okay and an asshole is history." James stood up and paced in front of the Frank's desk. "That ain't necessarily bad news." The sergeant changed back to the subject at hand, "This phantom shitter thing is going to be wrapped up by this time tomorrow morning. And as far as the guys doing the break in, the worst they can do is to send us to prison. I can do a nickel in the joint easy if I thought I could get back on motors and out of SIU."

"Thanks for cheering me up. Now go piss up a rope."

Hank tried again, "Hell, a judge approved it."

Bailey gave his 'don't bullshit me' look. "He might have approved a break-in for a bug, but I don't think he wrote anything in the court order about Quintero shitting on the suspect's desk."

Hank sat back down, looking somewhat dejected that his impassioned speech had turned to shit.

Bailey took his feet off the desk and sat up. He appeared somewhat renewed. "You know Hank, you got a point."

"No I don't."

Bailey continued, "I got to stop feeling sorry for myself. We got a break on the case, Denise survived her shooting, and till they get all this damned thing straightened out, we will be eligible for retirement, screw 'em."

Hank seemed motivated again, except for the lingering confusion about what his point was.

"Let's go down to the listening post and find out what's going on. If we get enough, we arrest De Vincent-Milo and let God sort it all out."

Hank stood and adjusted his belt. "Solid," He said in tribute to Link, the hero of his youth.

The two men hustled out of the building, leaving the coffee pot to burn up its contents as usual.

***

Rowdy nervously worked on changing the tapes at the listening post as the first police officer arrived at De Vincent-Milo's office. He popped the fresh tape in the machine in time to hear Claire begin the confrontation.

"Well, it's about time!" Claire started the contact with her nose in the air.

"Ma'am I'm officer Drake. I understand there was a break-in."

Rowdy admired the officer's ability to maintain the cool exterior of professionalism as they listened to the bug. This officer is acting cool, he thought to himself, but inside I know he's thinking, 'You old bitch'.

Claire's voice got louder, "Not just a break-in, Mister. A terrorist attack on me for my political views. Obviously, the radicals don't want to see me running for higher office. Well, young man you can tell the American public that I call these criminals a pack of cowards and I spit in their eye. I shall run for higher office. The American people do not want to see their leaders run in the face of danger!" She pointed dramatically to the feces on her desk.

Drake mumbled, " I don't think the American people want to see this pile of shit on your desk either.

"What did you say?"

"I said, I don't think so either, ma'am."

"Young man, have you notified the Chief and the Public Information Officer yet?"

"Ma'am," He sounded confused. "Notified them of what?"

Claire's face turned beet red and she started shaking as she screamed in the young officers face, "GET YOUR GOD-DAMNED SERGEANT DOWN HERE NOW AND GET THE HELL OUT OF MY OFFICE!"

The officer said the words, "Yes, ma'am," but the tone of his voice said, "No problem."

***

At the listening post, Rowdy, Snort and Quintero giggled again. Snort actually held his nose to suppress his snickering and danced in a little circle like he just scored a touchdown.

Bailey and James came through the door and saw the overweight narc bending over and wiggling his butt as part of the victory dance.

James took one look at the exposed pimply, white butt crack and said, "Yuck!"

The detectives turned quickly at the sound of their supervisor's comment. Their facial expressions changed from giddy to serious as they all tried to appear sufficiently grim in respect to the serious nature of the investigation.

Bailey was the next to speak, "I take it Claire called the cops?"

Rowdy always considered himself the appropriate spokesperson for the brass, "Yes, sir." He pushed his glasses back up his nose with his index finger, instead of his middle finger as usual, out of respect. "It appears that the target has notified the officer of the serious nature of this violation."

James snickered, he had heard this bullshit before.

The Lieutenant raised his palm, "Okay, so the old bitch bit, right?"

Snort responded, "You can roger that, Skipper!"

"When are you going in?"

Quintero chimed in, "I shall take 'Larry the Lot Man' to the office in about an hour, then, if all goes well, Quintero will take him back in and hit her up for more money."

It always bothered Bailey that Quintero and Bob Dole talked about themselves in the third person all the time. "Okay, when she hits the ceiling, that should give us enough probable cause to nail the bitch beyond any shadow of a doubt." Bailey paused. "I want you guys to do this right. This is a political case and we are totally operating on our own."

The detectives nodded in understanding.

Bailey wrapped up the briefing, "Kick some ass and keep me posted."

Headquarters

Denise was dismissed by the shooting team. They didn't ask a lot of questions. They just looked around, took some notes and left. She knew most of them. They all had kids at home. They left her with the impression that a dead child molester didn't merit a lot of investigation, nobody gives a shit how he bought it, just as long as he's off the street for good.

Denise spent the next three hours waiting behind her desk at Headquarters for the division commander to call her in for the initial findings of the investigation. The phone rang and the commander requested her to come down to his office.

"Denise, I don't know the full details yet, but the shooting team said, 'no worries', so I guess that's good."

She wearily shook her head in agreement. She didn't hear what he said.

He handed her a phone number written on a blue sticky-note, "Call this guy, he's the contract shrink, and get an appointment. He has to give you a clearance to come back to work."

"Yes, sir." She looked vacantly ahead.

"You have three days paid leave coming to deal with this, then you're supposed to come back to work if the Doc signs off on you, okay?"

"Yes, sir," She agreed again, her voice lifeless.

He leaned forward in his chair, "And Denise, for what it's worth, you did the world a favor."

"Thank you, sir."

As she left Headquarters, several officers patted her on the back as she passed them in the hall. "Way to go. Good job." She heard them, but could only respond with a nod. She exited the building and headed to her car.

At the north parking lot she saw the LeBaron convertible that Bailey was assigned pulling into the side driveway. She stopped as the car circled the lot and pulled up to her.

Bailey stepped out and for a moment, they said nothing. "Denise, I'm sorry. I'm just glad you're okay."

She looked blankly at him, "I need to go home Frank. I know none of this was your fault, but I do need to go home."

Frank had seen the thousand yard stare before. He remembered seeing it in the mirror a long time ago. No matter how he felt, he knew Denise had to go home and deal with this. She was strong enough. She would get better. But not today.

He took a quick glance around the parking lot, then gave her a little hug. "Call me when..."

She nodded and walked off.

***

Denise entered her apartment and kicked off her shoes. After latching the door knob lock, securing the dead bolt, and hooking the security chain on the door behind her, she sat down in her favorite chair, the big overstuffed one where she could curl up and feel safe from the world. She let herself cry a little, gathered her thoughts, and decided not to be a victim any more.

She got up and walked into the kitchen. Grabbing handful of tissue from the box on the counter, she blew her nose. She dabbed at her nose as she crossed the room, opened the refrigerator and grabbed a carton of wine coolers. On her way out she disconnected the phone and headed for the bath tub.

***

CHAPTER 31

Claire frantically dialed up talk radio stations trying to get someone interested in interviewing her about her terrorist attack, only to find that a state senator had been arrested for hiring a prostitute on Van Buren Street in Phoenix, and her story just wasn't that hot. She threw the phone off the desk and sat with arms crossed, her chin trembling in frustration.

Unexpectedly, Larry walked into her office carrying a small bag concealing a mini-cam. He rolled video and audio tape as he spoke. "Mrs. Milo, I came for the rest of the money."

She slowly looked up, her face showing the wear of being third class news. "I ain't paying you jack shit! Nobody cares. Now get out of here before I turn that damned tape of you stealing shit over to the police." She dismissed him with a wave of the hand.

"Wait a minute lady, we did the break-in, we shit on the desk. If I don't get the rest of the money, I'm going to get my ass kicked by the other guy."

Claire snarled, "Get out. NOW!"

Larry sauntered out to the street and got in the waiting tow truck.

***

Snort got on the radio, "We're clear."

Rowdy looked up at Quintero, "The snitch didn't get enough incriminating statements for a bust. You're on, daddy-o."

Quintero slowly turned his head, the rest of his body motionless, as he replied in his deepest monster voice with a monotone, "Cool."

***

At quarter to eight in the morning, Denise soaked in a steaming bubble bath. The warm soapy water relaxing her and releasing the tension of the shooting. Her mind drifting, she recalled the stress management lecture at the academy and permitted herself a smile.

"I hope I don't go mental or something and start maniacally scrubbing myself to remove the guilt," she told a soap bubble as she popped it with her toe.

The only problem was, she didn't feel guilty. As a matter of fact, it actually felt good to rid the earth of that piece of scum.

Denise felt a sense of release from the mental torture of her own childhood experience that drove her to be a cop. Capping that maggot evened up the score.

Like Snort and the other guys in SCAT are always saying, she thought, "Fuck 'em in the heart."

She stepped out of the tub and toweled off. She crawled into bed and slept more soundly than she had in years.

Breakfast

Bailey and James sat at Orlando's restaurant eating pancakes and saying little. They both knew that this was going to be a hell of a day, maybe they would both get fired.

Hank swallowed a bite and asked, "Is Denise going to be okay?"

Bailey cut up a pancake with his fork and knife, chopping the whole thing to bits before he ate it, "Nobody knows the answer to that, not even Denise." He took a bite and continued with his mouth full, "I hope so. I'll try and call her later."

Hank disagreed, "I think you should send Mutha over. She is the best unlicensed psychiatrist this side of Lake Erie."

Bailey raised an eyebrow at the geographical reference, then remembered that Hank was from Michigan. "I'm ahead of you Kemo Sabe. Mutha already spent some time with her and she thinks it will all be okay. Denise is tougher than she looks."

Changing subjects again, he lamented, "I hope those guys don't fuck this up."

"They probably will." Hank poured another half of a bottle of syrup on his cakes.

"Yeah, but you know what? I would never say this in front of anybody else, but it is kind of fun working with Quintero again." Bailey reluctantly admitted.

"That's the truth, Boss. I ain't seen this much excitement since the hogs ate Granny."

***

Old Buck Nelson, the security guard at Claire's office did a double-take when he saw the man walking across the parking lot. "What in the heck?"

The man had a ghetto blaster as big as a Volkswagen balanced on his right shoulder blaring out some heavy metal music so loud that the guard felt the bass sound vibrating in his chest.

"Oh, my God." Buck realized that the weirdo turned sharply and was heading right for him. The guard's hand started shaking and he unsnapped his holster as the stocky figure approached the door he was supposed to be protecting.

"What do I do? What do I do?" He tried to memorize a description to give to the police, if the guy didn't kill him first; Okay, he looks about six foot four inches tall, multi-colored shirt, black full length spandex bicycle pants, and purple Army boots.

As the subject drew nearer, he could make out the tattooed sketch of Adolph Hitler on the guy's shaved head. He could also make out the writing on the big cowboy belt buckle adorning the weight lifting belt around his waist, *'This is my fucking belt'* imprinted around a skull and cross bones.

"Oh, my, oh my!" Buck saw the guy wasn't wearing a multi-colored shirt. He had graffiti spray painted all over his bare upper torso!

"SHIT!"

The guy stopped about six inches from the guards nose and punched a button on the Ghetto blaster, pausing the earth shaking music and creating an eerie moment of silence.

"Go take a break, or I'll fuck you in the butt," the strange figure said in a slow monotone.

The guard decided, no big decision to make here for six bucks an hour, break time it was.

As the guard ran out, Quintero went in, flipping on the bug transmitter and tape recorder concealed in the stereo.

Outside the Dealership
Surveillance Team

Snort provided cover, waiting in the tow truck around the corner. Rowdy manned the monitoring station. Bailey and James sat in a car down the street from Snort, snickering as they got updates on the secure SIU radio channel from Rowdy.

Snort broke in on the channel. "A security guard just came out of the dealership hauling ass... He's running down the street westbound, he's trying to pull something out of his pocket... It's cool, just car keys... He's shaking like a dog shittin' a peach pit. Okay. He's getting in a car... Looks like a faded red '72 Pinto. He's pulling out...He's hauling ass westbound on Main at top speed, maybe forty or forty-five miles an hour."

James looked at Bailey quizzically, "I wonder what that was all about?"

Bailey tried to suppress laughter, "You used to work with the crazy bastard too, what do you think happened?"

"I think he either kissed him on the mouth or scared the living shit out of him."

Bailey couldn't stop laughing at the thought of it, "Probably both."

CHAPTER 32

Quintero fed on the look of surprise, disgust, then fear on the face of Claire De Vincent-Milo as he stepped unannounced through her office, throwing the double entry doors open like a gunfighter walking into a western saloon.

"What the hell do you want?" she scooted back in her chair.

"I either want my money or I want my shit back!" He hadn't blinked once since he came in the building. He stared at her with bugging eyes. The pulsing vein in his forehead made the Hitler tattoo look like blood was pumping through the fascist's carotid artery.

She started to reach for the phone but Quintero stepped forward and put his hand over hers, leaning over her desk, close enough for her to feel his hot breath on her face.

"You are the one that hired Larry to hire me to shit on the desk, are you not?" He droned in baritone.

Claire started shaking, "Yeah, but I figured he paid you. How much do you want!" Fear of being the victim of a Manson-style mutilation overwhelmed her business sense.

"Fifty dollars more."

Her small leather change purse sat on the desk and she reached in an pulled out a hundred dollar bill. She shoved the bill into his hand, "Take it and get out of here for God's sake."

He closed his fist around the money but didn't move. "I said fifty, not one hundred. I am not a thief."

Claire screeched, "I don't know what the hell you are! Just take it!"

Quintero still didn't move. Claire started squirming as he stood there staring at her, unblinking, not saying a word.

Suddenly, he spoke again, "Fine."

He turned his back in a snappy about face and headed for the door. He heard Claire exhale a sigh of a relief. Quintero stopped and slowly looked back over his shoulder, paused, then lifted his left leg and ripped a fart so powerful it caused a ripple wave in his bicycle pants.

"Your change, Madame."

Claire fainted.

***

CHAPTER 33

Officer Tina Cromwell, a seven year veteran, arrived at the scene of the unknown trouble call at the office of Vice-Mayor Archwald. She had been on the street long enough to see a lot, but she wasn't quite prepared for this one. The sobbing secretary, who had unlocked Archwald's office at eight-thirty to leave a memo on his desk, found him. Tina looked around the room from the doorway, not wanting to enter a possible homicide scene, leaving the distraught secretary in the reception area.

The odor of human feces, all over the top of the desk, almost made her gag. The Vice-Mayor lay on the floor, his neck at an odd angle and his head laying in a pool of blood emanating from his mouth and ears. His eyes were open and glazed. His pants and underwear were around his ankles.

Tina pushed the door closed and put her arm around the secretary. "I'm sorry ma'am, he's gone. Now why don't you sit down here and let me get some more help."

She directed the sobbing woman over to a small couch before getting on the radio and requesting her sergeant respond.

The tinny voice projected out of the radio speaker, "10-4, S-1227 will be responding from Headquarters."

Officer Cromwell punched the transmit button again, "Better send me one paramedic to come into the crime scene and make a death declaration. No need for a code three response."

***

Rowdy, Snort, and the two supervisors were still at the monitoring station, listening to the taped confrontation with Claire for the tenth time. Each playing of the tape resulted in more crude imitations and uncontrollable laughter.

***

Quintero drove to Headquarters and made a copy of the hundred dollar bill for the case file and placed it and the tape of his meeting with DeVincent-Milo in evidence.

Quintero was weird, but he was always a professional. He went into the Headquarters locker room and removed his fake Hitler tattoo and bizarre costume. He jumped into the shower and washed off the graffiti. He pulled his uniform out of the locker and completed the transformation back to beat officer.

Quintero went to the briefing room and churned out a report of the incident written in his usual exacting detail within an hour.

He made a copy of his completed report and stuffed it in an inter-office envelope for Bailey. He threw the original in the completed report basket and headed for the exit.

As he approached his patrol car in the parking lot, Quintero saw Sergeant Deeson, the dweeb, eyeballing him.

The nosy little worm probably wants to pump me for information about this case, Quintero thought. He stopped, pulling a pen out of his pocket and quickly made a couple of marks on his hand.

"Welcome back, Mr. Pepé ." He said in his deepest monotone.

"It's about time. Those SIU people are strange." Mister Pepé answered in the high squeaky voice.

Quintero suddenly turned his hand towards Deeson, who was walking in his direction.

The Pepé voice shouted in a piercing shriek, "Deeson... Deeson... Come and spank Mister Pepé's donkey!"

Deeson did an about face and fast walked back toward the station, acting like he was talking on his radio and doing his damnedest to avoid Quintero.

Mr. Pepé shrieked, "Deeson, come back, be my homosexual lover!"

Quintero smiled at the retreating Deeson, then whispered to his partner and confidant.

"Mr. Pepé, God help me, I love being a cop!"

Pepé replied enthusiastically, "Me to!"

***

James, Emma and Bailey sat in 'Guns and Buns' sipping coffee and munching on biscuits and gravy.

Sitting quietly, they let their muddled minds wander while enjoying the spicy breakfast and steaming bitter coffee that was the trademark of the diner.

Hank set his fork down and dabbed at his mustache with his napkin, cleaning up some gravy debris. "Frank, have you given any thought to pulling the pin?" We got two weeks and a wake-up call until we are off probation and the department goes on it. Twenty years! What are you going to do?"

"I think I'll wait until somebody pisses me off. I'll go then. It ain't like I'm in a hurry or anything."

Emma whined, "Being a civilian, I got another 13 years to do before I can get out."

Bailey and James wrinkled their noses at the mere sound of another 13 years.

"What are you going to do then, Mutha? All you know how to do is wet nurse psychotic cops." Bailey asked.

I'm planning on getting a job at a fat ladies' dress shop. I can get a salary and commission just for telling them they look good in that shit."

The two men nodded in approval of Emma's well thought out plan.

James piped in, "I'm staying twenty-five. Go out at 60%. Buy a motorcycle. Travel the country. You know I got to stay at least twenty-five. All those young police babes would be broken hearted if I left."

"I'm sure. It would be like losing their favorite grandpa."

"Fuck you very much, Frank. That hurt." Hank swallowed a small bite of biscuit. "It's too bad Denise has so long to do, you and her could have a good time running around. Seeing the sites. Before you get too old to enjoy it.

"Shit, I think I already am too old to enjoy it." Bailey grabbed the check, "I'll get it this time."

James pulled a buck out of his pants pocket. "I'll catch the tip."

Emma pulled a small daytimer out of her purse and started writing.

"What are you doing?" Hank asked.

"Making a note for my calendar. It's truly an historic event when you two clowns don't try to stiff me for the tab with some sob story about being broke."

Bailey and James started to whine, but Emma stared them down with her evil eye look that stopped any dissenters in their tracks.

***

CHAPTER 34

Sergeant Dick Tryon, homicide, stuck his head in the door for one quick look around Archwald's office. He stepped back out and took a deep breath. He walked out to his car and got a jar of Vicks Medicated Rub. Tryon filled his nostrils with the pasty substance to kill the effects of the odor.

He went back in the office and found the note, 'The king must be set free.'

"Pervert." Tryon knew sexual perversion when he saw it. He always suspected Archwald as a sicko, ever since the son-of-a-bitch pushed to cut the cost of living raise last year for the city employees. Tryon looked around the room long enough to pencil-whip out an initial report for his boss.

Headquarters - Chief's Office

Chief of Police Milquetoast Milton listened to the update, as the commander of the homicide unit explained the case status. He propped his feet up on his desk, grinning in sheer delight as he pondered the events of the preceding night.

"First of all Boss, that shooting with the little female detective was as righteous as can be. She shot a child molester, incidentally he was white so no problems with the local media. Anyway, she capped him right while he was in the act of molesting some little kid. She ought to get a medal of valor for that one.

"Damned straight she'll get the medal of valor. I'll pin it on her myself. Female detective, too. Thanks to my affirmative action programs, she was there at the right place at the right time. Do I know how to manage a police department, or what?"

The commander nodded emphatically, "You sure do, sir." He took a deep breath and laid out the big deal of the morning. "As you know, Vice-Mayor Archwald was found dead in his office. Evidence indicates he died during some type of strange sexual ritual. Also, it appears as though he was the one who defecated on the Mayor's desk. The poor devil must have gone off the deep end."

The Chief looked stunned, "My God, Archwald?"

"I'm afraid so, sir. The evidence is overwhelming. A similar note was found and the M.O. is well... unique to say the least."

The Chief wanted to laugh, one more asshole out of the way to his bid for Mayor. "That's a shame."

"The truth is, sir, we're writing it up as a natural death and we'd like to close out the related case at City Hall, just to protect the city from any further embarrassment."

"Oh, absolutely, we must protect the city. Besides, there no sense in running a dead man's name through the mud." Milton tried to think of how he might leak this story to that free hippie newspaper that was always doing an exposé on political issues.

The Chief's reverie was interrupted by the secretary knocking softly on the door. "Lieutenant Bailey is here in the lobby, sir. He says he needs to brief you on the... uh, Mayor's case."

The Chief saw the Lieutenant through the doorway and motioned him in with an irritated little wave, "What is it, Bailey?"

"Sir, it's about this thing on the Mayor's desk..."

"I know, I know. General Investigation Division solved that one for you. I can't believe Slim Archwald was such a sicko. Well, you're off the hook this time. If there is nothing else, please excuse yourself, we have to deal with the Archwald thing."

"I'm sorry sir, who...?

"Vice-Mayor Archwald was the suspect. The man flipped out. Now that is all Lieutenant, good day."

***

Bailey walked out of the Chief's office in a daze. He thought, have I missed something there?

He pulled his cellular out of his jacket pocket and called Hank and the two narcs.

"Meet me for a briefing at the SIU office in half an hour. Something has come up."

***

"Gentlemen, no one seems to care about Claire De Vincent-Milo, and it appears that our 'buddy' at the city council, Slim Archwald is deader than a doornail and taking the rap. Not that it's a bad thing, it just leaves us with the question. 'Now what'?"

Snort looked disgusted, "Every time somebody dies, those General Investigation pussies start clearing paper behind them."

James interrupted, "What do you want us to do?"

"All I want you to do is to take all the reports, tapes, and evidence back to the judge who signed the court order for the wiretap on DeVincent-Milo's office and let's hope this thing blows over without anybody hearing about it again. I'm going home and get some sleep."

***

At about eight P.M. Denise called Frank at home and woke him up. "Were you asleep?"

"That's okay. I should get up. How are you? I was worried." Frank wiped the sleep from his eyes and tried to focus on his clock radio.

She giggled, "You're in bed, aren't you?"

"Yeah."

"Stay right there. That's exactly where I want you."

Frank was too tired to think up a cool reply, "Good."

"And then, in the morning, we can talk about the future." She disconnected.

Bailey put the phone back in the cradle. He had a pretty good idea what she meant by that comment about the future. "Oh no, not again." He picked up the bottle of aspirins from the night stand and threw a handful in his mouth. *I'll be paying alimony with social security checks.*

The Crime Lab

Adolph Von Hammel labored over his lab table slowly examining the specimen from the Mayor's desk. As he carefully pushed it with a wooden tongue depressor, he noted that the paper it was deposited on was one of those super market tabloids. He was amazed that after all this time you could still read the print. 'Vanna White - a Devil Worshipping Lesbian?' accompanied with an unflattering photograph.

He shook his head in disbelief, These Americans, he thought, are an interesting people, ja.

***

CHAPTER 35

Bailey's Apartment

Denise seemed different since the shooting. Although she was always an upbeat person, she seemed more happy and playful lately. Bailey liked the change.

They sat on the sofa at his apartment and watched an old John Wayne movie about the cavalry and sipped on wine coolers. Bailey flipped through a sailing magazine and showed Denise a picture of a boat.

"This is one like the old guy I was telling you about is selling."

Denise took the magazine and looked the photo over carefully. "The retired Captain from the PD?"

"Yeah, he was before your time, but he's selling the boat and his condo in Lake Havasu. He's moving in with his kids in Indianapolis."

"I love Havasu. I wish you had the money to buy it. Maybe you'd let me come and visit." She snuggled closer and gave him a little bite on the ear.

"Don't say anything to anybody, babe, but I have the money."

"What are you talking about. In the dictionary under broke, they got your picture."

"Not exactly."

"What are you talking about?" Denise sat up with a curious smile.

"Do you recall the friend of mine..." He paused as he considered how to phrase it, "Who... passed away a while back?

"Recall... you were so upset we almost broke up. You didn't want to see anybody, talk to anybody. Of course I remember."

"He uh... Left me everything. His insurance, home, truck. I never said anything to anybody because... You know what a bunch of assholes people can be. Anyway, I didn't know what to do with it."

"Frank Bailey, you are the most secretive man I have ever known." She laughed, then abruptly sobered when she saw how serious he was, "Frank, how much was it?"

"About a quarter of a million."

Denise went limp with shock and fell off the couch. "Frank, what are you going to do with it? Why are you still working here?"

"Just don't say anything to anybody. My twenty years on the PD is up soon and maybe then, if the timing is right, I'll decide what to do. But mainly, I want to use it in a way to at least... I don't know, a way that would make Joe Trenton happy, maybe give me and Joe both some peace."

"What do you have in mind?"

"A little experiment I've been thinking about. I'd like to answer the question, Is there life after police work."

Superior Court Building - Maricopa County

Snort walked up the steps to the Maricopa County Superior Court with the tapes and reports in his arms stuffed in a couple of paper grocery sacks. The burly undercover cop pushed his way through the crowd and got on the elevator.

The occupants of the elevator car took one glimpse of the detective's dirty long hair, black leather jacket, and Harley-Davidson baseball cap and quickly exited. He rode alone to the 11th floor to the chambers of the judge who signed the wiretap order for them.

As he walked through the doors of the outer office an elderly clerk reached for the phone. Snort was used to the reaction, "Sorry ma'am, no need to call security, I'm an officer." He set his burden down and pulled out the badge, suspended by a small chain under his T-shirt.

"Parma City PD, Detective Murphy. I'm returning materials from an ex-parte order to the Judge."

The clerk's voice gave hint of relief. "Oh, of course Detective. The judge was expecting you. Please go in."

Snort picked up his sacks as the clerk announced him on an intercom. He walked through the big wooden doors and set the packages down on the dark brown leather chair in front of the antique oak desk. He stood at something resembling attention and addressed the Judge, who busily scribbled something on his notepad.

"Your Honor, I ain't sure what to do in situations like this, but no one seems to give a shit about this case." Snort handed the judge a thin file.

The judge, a distinguished looking gentleman with a thick head of silver gray hair and dark blue eyes, smiled as he reviewed the initial synopsis at the head of the first page.

"The folks at party headquarters are going to love this!" he mused.

"Excuse me?"

"Nothing, Detective. Just thinking out loud."

The Judge smiled at the newly delivered opportunity. De Vincent-Milo had been a thorn in their side for years, raising funding for all the liberal asshole candidates and their stupid 'Save the World' causes. Now they had the bitch by the short hairs.

The judge leaned back in his chair and propped his feet on the corner of his desk. "Detective Murphy, you've been coming in here with narcotics cases and special operations for how long now?"

"I don't know Judge, maybe twelve years." Snort started squirming, suspecting an ass-chewing coming.

"You are probably no great fan of the subject in this matter, I would presume, based on her adversarial relationship with the police. Am I correct?"

Snort appeared confused. "Do you mean, do I think she's a commie bitch like Hanoi Jane?"

The Judge spun his chair away from Snort, concealing a grin. "Let me put it this way, Detective. Would you be happy if Mrs. De Vincent-Milo left town and retired to Florida, never to be heard from again?"

"Yes, sir. I mean, I don't want her to get killed or nothing particularly. I mean, unless she just dies or something, which I wouldn't lose any sleep over, but..." Snort leaned over the desk and whispered conspiratorially, "She ain't no friend of the cop on the street, if you know what I mean."

"I understand completely Detective. Have a nice day."

Snort Murphy walked out of the building in a state of bewilderment. Like a big bear, he lumbered across the street to his tow truck. He paused long enough to rip a parking ticket off his windshield and tear it up before hopping in the truck's cab.

Snort sat behind the wheel in deep thought as he tried to cipher out what had just occurred in the judge's chambers. Suddenly, a smile crossed his homely face as he realized he just got that cranky old anti-police bitch kicked out of Dodge.

"God, I love this job." He fired up the engine and hurried back to Parma City to share the news with Rowdy.

CHAPTER 36

Bailey went through his morning routine of gathering his briefcase and bag of equipment out of his car to carry up to the office. He walked across the crowded parking lot when he glimpsed two old men who seemed to be arguing with a transient.

He came close enough to hear the transient saying he was fighting for his life due to an exposure of agent orange.

Bailey recognized the old men. It was the Mayor, and... Walter Hoskins the jumper? Bailey also recognized the transient was one of the regulars who Bailey had words with before.

"Mr. Mayor, is everything okay here?", Bailey eyed the bum as he spoke.

The transient did a quick about face and walked away.

"Oh yes, just fine. Oh, you're young Mr..."

"Bailey, sir. From the Police Department."

"Yes, of course. I'm sorry, my memory isn't what it used to be."

"That's quite all right, sir. Was that man bothering you?"

"No, not really. We were just coming from my office. I gave Mr. Hoskins here a citizenship award for fighting drugs in the community."

Hoskins interrupted, "I keep trying to tell you Mayor, I didn't fight him, I fell on him."

The Mayor continued, "While we were walking by, that young man gave us this note. It reminds me of one I got someplace before but I just can't remember." He handed the note to Bailey.

Bailey glanced at the note then did a double take, 'The King must be set free'. He looked around the lot, but the transient had disappeared.

Bailey folded the note and put it in his pocket. "Maybe you would like to visit the Narcotics Unit office and have a cup of coffee Mr. Mayor and Mr. Hoskins?"

Hoskins replied, "What floor is it on?"

"Never mind, let's find your car."

CHAPTER 37

Police Headquarters
Chief's Office

"Bailey, this is the last straw." The Chief leaned across his desk and pointed a finger at the Lieutenant's face. "Mister, your people are out of control. Another excessive force complaint..."

"He shot at us first..."

"And another rudeness complaint..."

"From the president of a motorcycle gang?"

"And not one of the buy money sheets balanced for the third month in a row!"

"Accounting was never my forté, sir."

Milton slammed his fist on the desk, "I'm sick and tired of SIU unit problems and you are damned well going to fix it."

"Chief, do you know what today is?"

Milton's face turned redder, "What is that supposed to mean?"

"It means, sir, that I have my twenty years in today and I am formally advising you of my retirement, effective the end of the month."

Milton sat back in his chair, stunned. "Frank, are you sure you're not being hasty, I mean, without your expertise, who else is going to run SIU? Hell, those cases are complicated. Who else can control that bunch of wild men over there?"

Frank turned and walked toward the door, "I'm sure it will all work out Chief. You'll find somebody. That young Sergeant Deeson is on the promotional list. He's your kind of guy."

"Deeson? DEESON! That guy is a fucking retard, for crying out loud!"

Bailey looked over his shoulder as he walked out the Chief's door for the last time. "Exactly my point, sir."

"What the hell is that supposed to mean?" Milton was out of his chair, following Bailey down the hall.

Bailey stopped and put a hand out keeping the agitated Milton at arm's length. "It means this, if you have even the slightest clue about the working of this department, you will check your promotion list and find that Sergeant Hank James is number three on the list. He's senior to the number one and two goofs who beat him out on the test. Since Hank is a soul brother, you can get away with promoting him now. Hell, he's the most qualified man!"

"What do you mean.. soul brother?"

"He's black, Chief... Sergeant James is an African-American."

"Oh. One of those."

"And arguably the finest man you have working for you, unless he decides to retire too...then, I guess there *is* Deeson."

"Oh my."

Bailey condescendingly put his hand on the shoulder of the man who could no longer cause him stress. "Chief, good luck." He paused, "I sincerely wish I meant it."

***

Chief Milton skulked back to his desk, furious at the insubordinate Bailey. "Asshole. He'll regret it. It's tough out there in the real world." The Chief flopped down in his oversize executive chair and threw a handful of Tums in his mouth. He chewed them to a chalky powder then pulled the Maalox out of a desk drawer and slugged down half of a bottle to wash the tablets down with.

The Chief muttered between gulps "That arrogant bastard. He had to be stealing dope or something. I never did trust him. Not a team player. Asshole."

Milton hit his intercom button and summoned his secretary, " Get me the personnel file on Sergeant James... I think the first name is Chuck or Pete or something like that. Bring in my confidential file, too. And get the Lieutenant board promotion committee up here. It looks like we have an opening."

He hit the button again shutting off the little intercom on his phone.

"Asshole, Bailey, now I have to promote this damned colored guy."

Milton started to stand up, but froze as he felt what seemed like a blow from a sledge hammer to the center of his chest. The force of the spasm caused the Chief to lurch back in his chair, grasping his chest with both hands. He fell to the floor, eyes bulging out like a dead salmon. He never uttered his final words.

Downtown

Lieutenant, soon to be civilian, Frank Bailey walked out of Headquarters with his independence and a wide smile, "You know," he said to no one in particular, "That really felt good." He lit a cigarette. "Really, really good!"
He ignored the ambulances rolling up to the building as he crossed the street to the parking garage, dismissing them as the routine Fire Station One rescue call for whiny jailbirds claiming police brutality.

Bailey walked into the office suite of the SIU and squared his chin to make the announcement. He stepped into the center of the room and started to speak when he was interrupted by a red eyed, spastic Emma Flanagan.

She pulled a tissue from the box on her desk and dabbed at her eyes, "What the hell did you do, Frank?" She sounded more like an accusing ex-wife than an old friend and peer.

A confused Bailey tried to answer, "Just what I always said I'd do, Emma. I didn't expect to upset you."

She wailed, "Oh my God, it's premeditated! Frank, shut up before they give you the fucking chair for God's sake!"

Bailey looked around the area and noticed the whole staff was distraught. "What fucking chair? They usually give you a plaque or a watch or something."

"Not for killing the god-damned Chief they don't!" replied Emma between sobs.

Frank stared wide-eyed. "What do you mean, killing the Chief?"

"The receptionist for the fourth floor just called me and said he had a meeting with you and then they found him dead in his office. My lord Frank, the man was an asshole, but you didn't have to kill him."

Frank couldn't generate a response.

Emma continued rattling on, "Oh don't try to deny it. I always knew this would happen. You and your damned Rush Limbaugh Republican testosterone!"

"Emma, all I did was tell him I was going to retire. I didn't kill the ignorant bastard. I should have, but I don't give a shit. In a week and a half, I'm a civilian again. I'm serious."

Emma didn't let up, "Oh, I know the bastard deserved it, the way he treated our SIU people, hell, the way he treated everybody... But why you Frank, why did you do it?"

Frank turned his palms up in a signal of surrender, recalling that Emma just quit smoking again. "For crying out loud Emma, I just told him I was retiring and that he ought to have Hank replace me!" He wondered if she was suffering from PMS, too. If she is, he thought, I'm dead too.

"I should have known that Hank was involved in this, and probably Quintero." The phone rang interrupting her. Her voice instantly changed back to the professional tone and demeanor as she answered the phone, "Sal's Cargo and Transit, how may I help you?"

Frank began looking for an escape route when he heard Emma utter a series of Oh.. Oh... ohs." He sensed the truth was on the line and decided to stick it out.

Emma put the phone down and slouched into her chair, "Frank, I'm so sorry. It's just... I don't know..."

Frank pulled a cigarette out of his shirt pocket and put it in her mouth, then reached over the top of her desk and opened the lap drawer. He pulled out a bottle of Midol and put it on the desk in front of her. She stared at him for a second then took the pill, washing it down with some coffee while Frank fumbled with his lighter.

"Take a deep breath Emma." Frank said paternally.

"Thanks Boss, I needed that." She meekly replied.

"Emma."

"Yes, Frank?"

"What are you talking about?"

She took a long drag on the smoke. "Chief Milton collapsed and died in his office with some kind of heart attack."

"Holy shit!" Frank lit up, too. What the hell, he wasn't a cop much longer anyway. Internal affairs wouldn't be able to complete the paperwork for the smoking violation before he was gone. Besides, this was deep shit.

"The new receptionist up in administration thought you were with him right before his secretary found him and she jumped to conclusions. Apparently he had asked for some files after you were gone."

"Oh."

"Sorry."

"Forget it. Want to go have a drink?"

"Definitely."

"Let's go."

She paused as she started to get up to leave, "Are you really retiring?"

"I am, Emma. My only regret is leaving SIU... And you."

Bailey was feeling kind of like a Humphrey Bogart. He paused for his hug and kiss.

"Asshole deserter."

Shit. That image didn't last long. Now Bailey felt like Bailey again.

"Let's go."

CHAPTER 38

Chapel of Peace Funeral Home

Snort and Rowdy sat in the last row of pews with Henderschott, James and Downey. They feigned listening to the eulogy as they passed a small bag of Gummy Bears back and forth.

City Manager Gilmore spoke eloquently about the Chief's service to the community as though he actually believed it.

"This brave man's last request was to make sure the department moved forward into the next century with minority officers sharing command, ensuring the city reflected the make-up of its citizens. He died at his desk working on promotions of minority officers, as a true leader and man of the community. An icon of affirmative action."

Henderschott whispered to James, "I thought you said he was a racist asshole?"

James shook his head. "No, just a regular asshole. He wasn't particularly racist, he just didn't care for black people."

Henderschott looked quizzically at James, "Excuse me?"

Downey elbowed and 'shushed' him. "Forget it, it's a black thing."

James snickered quietly. "Naw, it's a blue thing. Cops hate everybody equally. The Chief just wasn't a real cop."

Rowdy and Snort nodded energetically in agreement as the City Manager droned on about his own accomplishments.

"As I lead this city into the new millennium, I will take every possible opportunity to promote opportunity for minorities and the homeless and... other people in the legacy of our departed Chief...uh..." Gilmore looked like he lost his train of thought. "uh... Milton."

Downey leaned across Henderschott and asked James a whispered question, "Well, at least this paid off for you, being a minority or homeless or other, didn't it?"

James leaned across the other side of Henderschott, "Personnel said the city budgeted for three Lieutenant positions to be approved for the end of the month anyway. I hope these dick heads don't tear a rotator cuff patting themselves on the back for being Martin Luther Kings. The only thing this whole fiasco accomplished was holding up the promotion I earned until they can schedule a big media presentation at council chambers in three weeks. These assholes actually pushed my promotion back a week."

Denise was surprised, "Really?"

James grabbed another Gummy Bear out of the bag. "I'm sorry to say, it's true. Are you surprised?"

"No. It sounds like the city."

Gilmore's eulogy speech was sounding more and more like a Gilmore campaign speech as he blabbed about his support of law enforcement and civil rights.

James had heard enough and quietly left, followed by the other officers in the row.

They gathered outside the church and huddled for more small talk.

Hank asked, "Denise, have you seen Frank?"

"I wish I had, he took some vacation time and got out of Dodge the day after Milton croaked. Said he had all the bullshit one human being could deal with, packed his stuff in a truck, and headed for Lake Havasu."

Snort interrupted, "Cool."

"Yeah, I'm going to give him some time to settle in. I might drive over there for the weekend and go see him next month... Or whatever." Her voice took a melancholy tone.

Rowdy became enthused, "Maybe we could all go, make it a road trip!"

James smacked him on the back of the head with an open palm and Snort gave him a sneer. "Maybe they'd like to be alone you insensitive dick-head."

"Yeah, we'll see. I better go." Denise walked away with her head down as the little group of pseudo-mourners broke up.

James passed by the news crew as he walked to his car. He heard a reporter comment about the officers who were too overcome with grief to sit through the services for their fallen hero, having to gather to consoles themselves in the parking lot.

"I love this job. Like a kick in the nuts." he muttered as he crossed the parking lot.

EPILOGUE

Frank looked into her eyes as they stood on the bow of his sailboat, anchored off the shore of Lake Havasu City. The weather on the Arizona - California border lake provided for a perfect spring evening. Denise held his hand as they watched the setting sun change the hills on the California side of the lake to a deep purple. Frank pulled a match out of the pocket of his cotton slacks and lit a small candle on the deck. He stared out into the horizon as the small flame flickered in the fading light.

She brushed her fingers across his face, then drew him closer to her. "You know something Frank, you're a lot nicer guy since you retired. I think it's time for you to tell me, what made you finally decide to do it?" She gave him her soft smile and a nibble of a kiss on the ear.

He didn't respond for a few minutes as he turned his gaze back toward the sunset, contemplating how he would answer her.

He stepped back from her and said, "The time was right, it wasn't fun anymore. And like I told you, I had to know if there really is life after police work."

"Is there?" She asked.

He took a deep breath before answering. "I thought moving out here away from the city with the boat and condo would give me the answer, but there was still something ... missing."

He turned towards her and took her hands in his. He started to speak again but stopped as he searched for the right words.

She looked at him with sadness, feeling his discomfort. "Like what, Frank? What's missing?"

Frank let go with his right hand and gently tugged Denise's wallet badge from the pocket of faded blue Nautica jacket she wore. He flipped it open. The sun's final ray of evening glared off the metal shield before disappearing behind the hills. He ran his thumb over the cold metal surface of the detective shield.

"You have ten years on the department now Denise, that will give you a pension. And people say two can live as cheaply as one. I guess what I'm saying... asking is..."

She softly interrupted, "Should I consider this a proposal Frank?"

"Yeah, I think that's exactly what it is."

Denise didn't speak. As he held her in his arms, she kissed him softly, then passionately before pushing away. Gazing into his eyes, Denise took the badge from Frank's hand and gently tossed it overboard.

The soft splash in the cold blue darkness gave Frank the answer Joe Trenton never found.

The end

About the Author

Daniel retired in 1995 from a law enforcement career spanning 23 years. He currently manages his consulting firm, writes, and teaches criminal investigation courses at a local community college.

During his career as a peace officer he worked as a deputy sheriff in Darke County, Ohio and as a police lieutenant in Arizona. He is a certified defensive tactics instructor and a graduate of the DEA Drug Unit Commander's Academy. Dan received numerous awards and commendations for his work in drug raids, vice investigations, and tactical apprehensions. He graduated from the University of Phoenix in 1988.

Through his company, Sierra West Consulting, Dan develops training programs and manuals for law enforcement special operations units. He also enjoys addressing writers' groups concerning technical advice on police operations and police personalities. He is often available for law enforcement related fund raising activities.

Dan appreciates, based on first hand experience, the frustrations and joys of working undercover. Please visit the corporate web page at sierrawestbooks.com. For information on law enforcement training seminars or speaking engagements contact:

Sierra West Consulting, Inc.
602-964-6390 or outside of Arizona call toll free
1-888-860-1177

ORDER FORM

	PRICE	QUANTITY	TOTAL
Mason's Cav Border of Vengeance	$12.95		
Narc in the Dark	$14.95		
Legendary Lawmen	$14.95		
Pepper Spray Primer	$9.95		
Tall Tales of Queen Creek	$6.95		
		Shipping add $3.00 per item Az. Residence add 7% tax	
		Total	

Mail your check or money order to:
Sierra West Books
P. O. Box 8310
Mesa, Arizona 85214-8310